A MARKED BEE?

"Do you still want me to send them to Linka? I understand if you don't."

"Do you think they're safe?"

"I just examined the other r[...] one bee. And he's dead. I mean 's[...] paw and showed Hermux the bo[...]

Hermux took it from her gingerly. "My goodness. It's big, isn't it?"

"I would say extremely big."

Hermux turned it over. Its abdomen showed some curious markings. Hermux removed his magnifying loupe from his vest pocket. He opened it and fixed the lens to his eye. He held the bee close and examined it. The fur on the bee's belly seemed to grow in a distinct pattern. To Hermux it looked as though two letters were spelled out in golden hairs amongst the black. He squinted for better focus. They definitely appeared to be letters. "An I," he thought. "And an M." He showed them to Mrs. Thankton.

"How peculiar," he said. "What do you think that means?"

"I have no idea. Do you suppose it could be some sort of message?"

ALSO BY MICHAEL HOEYE

Time Stops for No Mouse
A HERMUX TANTAMOQ Adventure™

The Sands of Time
A HERMUX TANTAMOQ Adventure™

No Time Like Show Time
A HERMUX TANTAMOQ Adventure™

Time to Smell the Roses

A Hermux Tantamoq Adventure®

Michael Hoeye

PUFFIN BOOKS

PUFFIN BOOKS
Published by the Penguin Group
Penguin Young Readers Group, 345 Hudson Street, New York, New York 10014, U.S.A.
Penguin Group (Canada), 90 Eglinton Avenue East, Suite 700, Toronto, Ontario, Canada M4P 2Y3
(a division of Pearson Penguin Canada Inc.)
Penguin Books Ltd, 80 Strand, London WC2R 0RL, England
Penguin Ireland, 25 St Stephen's Green, Dublin 2, Ireland (a division of Penguin Books Ltd)
Penguin Group (Australia), 250 Camberwell Road, Camberwell, Victoria 3124, Australia
(a division of Pearson Australia Group Pty Ltd)
Penguin Books India Pvt Ltd, 11 Community Centre,
Panchsheel Park, New Delhi - 110 017, India
Penguin Group (NZ), 67 Apollo Drive, Rosedale, North Shore 0632, New Zealand
(a division of Pearson New Zealand Ltd)
Penguin Books (South Africa) (Pty) Ltd, 24 Sturdee Avenue,
Rosebank, Johannesburg 2196, South Africa

Registered Offices: Penguin Books Ltd, 80 Strand, London WC2R 0RL, England

First published in the United States of America by G. P. Putnam's Sons,
a division of Penguin Young Readers Group, 2007
Published by Puffin Books, a division of Penguin Young Readers Group, 2008

1 2 3 4 5 6 7 8 9 10

THE LIBRARY OF CONGRESS HAS CATALOGED THE G. P. PUTNAM'S SONS EDITION AS FOLLOWS:
Hoeye, Michael.
Time to smell the roses : a Hermux Tantamoq adventure / Michael Hoeye.
p. cm.
Summary: While immersed in wedding plans, Hermux is hired to find the son
of the patriarch of the DeRosenquill rose dynasty and in the process
discovers a homeless teenager, fields of dying flowers, and killer bees.
ISBN 978-0-399-24490-2 (hc)
[1. Mice—Fiction. 2. Animals—Fiction. 3. Missing persons—Fiction.
4. Mystery and detective stories.] I. Title.
PZ7.H67148Tm 2007 [Fic]—dc22 2007008200

Puffin Books ISBN 978-0-14-241243-5

Printed in the United States of America

For
RICHIE WILLIAMSON
Master Storyteller,
Artist & Magician

ACKNOWLEDGMENTS

Thank you to Martha Banyas, my love, my wife, my muse, and my pal, for listening and reading with unlimited patience and good cheer. Thank you to Nancy Paulsen, my marvelous, wise editor, for being able to keep the forest and the trees in sight at all times.

Many thanks to Ray Peck and Lisa Millikin at Wind Horse Coffee in Milwaukie, Oregon, for the best coffee and donuts outside of Pinchester. Thanks to the Women Walkers of Milwaukie (Betty, Darlene, Jean, Kathy, Kathy, Ricky, and Sue, plus Bob) for their morning cheer and support. Thanks to Shari Schaffer and the Literary Ladies of Bristow, Virginia, for their kind words when it really mattered. And thanks most of all to you, dear reader, for the generous use of your time.

CONTENTS

Chapter 1
THE WAR OF THE ROSES

"I had no idea that getting married was so much work." Hermux Tantamoq put his pen down and took a sip of coffee.

Nip didn't answer. He was reading the paper.

"Proposing was scary," Hermux went on. "But it was over in a second. This wedding business goes on and on. Look at all these lists of things to do! When am I supposed to work?" Hermux Tantamoq was a professional watchmaker, and good watchmaking required time and energy.

Nip reached for a donut and kept right on reading.

"A lot of decision-making goes into a wedding," Hermux continued. "More than you think."

Hermux waited, but Nip ignored him. "Listen to this!" Nip said. "Front page!"

UNIDENTIFIED BODY FOUND ON BEACH

Ceremony in Rose Capital Ends in Chaos— Victim Probably Drowned

THORNY END, June 5—The body of an unidentified squirrel washed to shore today, disrupting a crowded celebration in this seaside community. The grisly discovery took place as local dignitaries unveiled plans for restoring the Old Clocktower, a historic landmark that overlooks Thorny End's wholesale rose market.

"I thought it was just a small log at first," said Mayor Tattin Arffleck. "Then the waves rolled it over, and I saw it had a tail and eyes. Or it used to. It was horrible."

The body was transported by ambulance to the county morgue. An autopsy is pending to determine the cause of death.

Mayor Arffleck pooh-poohed the possibility of foul play. "It was obviously an accident. We don't get much crime hereabouts. We're too busy growing roses and living normal lives like normal people were intended to."

The mayor assured residents that plans for the clocktower will continue on schedule. Funds to repair the clock will be provided by DeRosenquill & Son, the world's

2

largest grower of premium roses. Founded over a century ago, the company still maintains its headquarters at the fabled Villa DeRosenquill in Thorny End.

The clocktower will be renamed in honor of Buddlin DeRosenquill, who was killed earlier this year in an automobile collision. Androse DeRosenquill, patriarch of the DeRosenquill family, was on hand to make the formal announcement. It was his first public appearance since the tragic death of his son.

(See related story on page 6.)

"Thorny End!" concluded Nip. "What do you think about that? Sounds like you better get down there!"

"What for?" asked Hermux. "I've got my hands full right here." Hermux glanced down at the list on the counter. Linka's note across the top read plainly: *I need this back <u>tomorrow</u> at the latest!*

It was already tomorrow. And he hadn't made much progress.

But Nip Setchley, Hermux's shop assistant, was on a mission. "Somebody's got to figure out whose body that is. And it doesn't sound like the mayor is going to be much help. Besides, that would be a big job, fixing that clock. Right up your alley! We could use a big job like that. And you could use the money, if I'm not mistaken."

Nip was right about that. Not only did weddings require plenty of planning, they required plenty of money too. Hermux pushed his list aside. Beneath it was Linka's first draft for their wedding budget. It would take a lot of broken alarm clocks to pay for all that. "All right. I'm listening. What's it say on page six?"

"Just this . . ."

REEZOR RULES!
THE FRESH PRINCE OF PERFUME BUILDS HIMSELF A MAGIC KINGDOM

A Moozella Corkin Exclusive

He's **Mr. Natural**. And he's on top of the charts. **Reezor Bleesom**'s smash hit, **Time to Smell the Roses**, continued its winning streak this week at fragrance counters across the country, bumping perennial sales champ **Tucka Mertslin** from the number-one slot.

We reached Reezor by telephone in Thorny End, where he is feverishly putting the finishing touches on his new country estate. "It's a dream come true!" said Reezor. "Thank you to all my fans. I couldn't have done it without

---

them. And I especially want to thank **Androse DeRosenquill** for trusting me to turn his masterpiece of a rose into a masterpiece of a perfume."

Reezor is so committed to **DeRosenquill & Son**'s flagship rose that he has planted one hundred acres of *Rosa fragrantissima*—**the King of Roses**®—to guarantee his factory a constant supply of priceless rose oil. "I use nothing but the best. And nothing but natural ingredients," he said. "Unlike some of my competitors."

And speaking of competitors, Tucka Mertslin wasted no time sending Reezor her warm personal congratulations. "These little successes are so important for somebody who's just starting out," she told us. "Personally, I can't see what the fuss is about 'all natural' perfume. Tucka Mertslin beauty products have always been 'all natural.' I made them, didn't I? And if I'm not a force of nature, who is?"

Reezor is throwing a star-studded party this Saturday to show off the new house and the rose garden, which will be at its peak. The theme is **"Life Is Just a Bed of**

Roses." And Reezor should know! Everyone who's anyone will be there, including me, naturally! And I'll fill you in on every fabulous rose-colored detail.

Time to Smell the Roses,
another "All Natural!® All the Time!®" fragrance from Reezor Bleesom, is available at Orsik & Arrbale.

Nip finished with a flourish. "See?"

"No," Hermux said. "I'm afraid I don't."

"Something's rotten in Thorny End. I wouldn't be surprised if that was Reezor Bleesom's body on the beach."

"Don't you think someone would have recognized him? Besides, he's a mouse. Remember? But I know what you mean. If I were Reezor, I'd watch my back. Tucka is not somebody you want as your enemy."

"I'd watch every direction." Nip reached for the donuts again but stopped midway. "Are you going to eat that toasted-coconut, cream-filled maple bar?"

"No. You eat it. I'm losing my appetite." Hermux yawned and gave his whiskers a good pull.

"Any progress on the list?"

"No. Still way too many names. And I just thought of somebody else." At the bottom of the list Hermux wrote, *Aunt Flanny.* Aunt Flanny wasn't really his aunt. But she was related somehow on his mother's side, and she would be terribly hurt if she didn't get an invitation to his wedding.

Linka wanted a small, intimate wedding for family and close

friends. Hermux didn't have much family, but he had a lot of friends and even more customers. And they all expected to be invited. They were already making suggestions about the menu and the band and especially the cake. Bratchlin Weffup, who was a very old and loyal customer, suggested setting up a suggestion box. Cladenda Noddem thought that was a splendid idea. She thought that Hermux should put the suggestion box right in the shop window so he could attract more suggestions. "You can never have too many good ideas!" she told him.

But Hermux thought that perhaps you could. And too many guests too. He was supposed to cut his list in half. And so far he hadn't crossed off a single name. His head throbbed. Maybe he was hungry after all. He reached for a donut. But Nip had taken the last one.

Just then the door opened and in marched Lista Blenwipple with the mail. She dumped a stack of envelopes and magazines on the counter.

"You're getting nowhere fast with that," she said, glancing at the list. "Give it to me."

Lista snatched the list away. She put on her reading glasses and removed a broad-tipped pen from her shirt pocket. Then she started from the top.

"Lanayda Prink?" she asked. "I thought this was going to be classy." She struck Lanayda's name off the list. "No. No. No. No. Not on your life." She crossed names off as fast as she could read. "You've got a lot of deadbeats here, Hermux. It's time to get real."

"I can't just not invite them!" Hermux tried to protest.

"Of course you can. Look how easy it is!" She crossed off six more names.

"But I've known these people my whole life."

"No reason to spoil a nice party." She saw her own name and nodded with satisfaction. "Linka's got the right idea. Small and intimate. We'll all have a better time. Frankly, if it was me, I wouldn't get married at all." Lista drew herself up. She turned coquettishly and raised her sensible skirt a notch to reveal a stocky but firm bit of leg for a middle-aged mouse. "And boys, it's not because I haven't been asked!" She twitched her tail suggestively.

Nip gulped.

"I can name names if you want," Lista teased. "But I don't want to shock you."

"No names," said Nip.

Lista finished her edit and returned the list to Hermux. He looked it over and saw social disaster speeding toward him like a freight train.

"Of course, as soon I'm gone, you can put those names back on," she told him. "But I can't guarantee their invitations will make it through the mail."

Chapter 2
THROUGH THICK AND THIN

For Tucka Mertslin the moment of truth came every day at 4:45, and it lasted for exactly fifteen minutes. That was about as much truth as Tucka could stomach in one sitting. Each afternoon she retired to her private dressing room in the executive suite at the world headquarters of Tucka Mertslin Cosmetics. There the most famous, the most beautiful, the most successful cosmetics tycoon on earth seated herself at her pink marble dressing table. She slowed her breathing, turned her vision inward, and cleared her mind of all the day's distractions. Then she counted to twenty-five before slowly opening her eyes to face her reflection in the mirror. Today the truth was good. She looked stunningly beautiful. Enormous, exotic eyes. Flawless furry cheeks. Black velvet muzzle. And lips that had launched a thousand lipsticks. But then Tucka's reverie was interrupted. Her hypercritical eye returned to her lips for a second look. She reached for her magnifying glass. She steeled herself for an unpleasant personal revelation.

And there it was. A truth she could no longer avoid. No matter how vivid the color or broad the stroke, lipstick could no longer conceal the fact that Tucka's lips were getting thin-

9

ner. She had built a fortune on youthful, voluptuous beauty, and there was nothing youthful or voluptuous about thin lips. She put down the glass. That was more than enough truth for one day. And there was still Clareen's report to get through. She pushed the intercom button.

"I'm ready," she told Clareen. "In case there's anything else." She paused, hoping that for once Clareen would say that she hadn't found anything. But that was not to be.

"I'll be right in," Clareen said brightly.

"I can't wait," said Tucka. While she did wait, she tried to make good use of her time, practicing her lip exercises. Pout, purse, pooch. Ten repetitions. Smile, smirk, smooch. Ten reps. Then repeat from the beginning. Before the third set Clareen arrived. Clareen Plagiste was Tucka's executive assistant and private secretary. She was smart, loyal, and thorough to a fault. She carried a dozen long-stemmed burgundy-red roses, a small bag from Orsik & Arrbale, and the afternoon paper. It was Clareen's task, and it was a thankless task to be sure, to gather the bad news of the day and present it to Tucka after her session with the mirror.

Tucka regarded Clareen drearily. "What's up?"

"Start here," Clareen said. She handed her the paper. She had opened it to Moozella Corkin's column and circled the headline in red crayon.

It was a good thing Tucka was sitting down. Reezor Bleesom, her former assistant and a textbook example of an ambitious, disloyal, ungrateful little worm, had finally done it. He was finally number one. He had pushed her from the top of the charts. It made her sick.

"And the flowers?" Tucka asked. Perhaps an admirer had sent them.

"These are the roses he's using. I thought you'd better smell them for yourself."

"How thoughtful. And the bag? A gift?"

Clareen shook her head. "It's time to smell the roses!" she said. She opened the Orsik & Arrbale bag.

Tucka's heart sank. "You didn't!"

"I did," said Clareen. "You have to face it eventually." She set a white box on Tucka's dressing table. On its side was a water-color painting of roses.

Time to Smell the Roses

EAU DE PARFUM
REEZOR BLEESOM FRAGRANCES
PINCHESTER
ALL NATURAL!® ALL THE TIME!®

"I'll leave you alone," Clareen said. She closed the door behind her softly.

Tucka sat motionless. She pushed the box away from her. She wasn't ready to face that just yet. She began with the roses instead. They were tied with satin ribbon. From the ribbon hung a gold medallion. On it was stamped a crown with the legend:

GENUINE ROSA FRAGRANTISSIMA—
the King of Roses® from the world-famous rose gardens of
DeRosenquill & Son, Thorny End

11

Tucka pulled a rose from the bouquet and with the sharp snuffle of a trained professional she inhaled its scent. "Delicious!" she muttered despite herself, then quickly added, *"If* you like obvious, beautiful smells." Unfortunately, she had to admit that that was exactly what most people *did* like, including herself. Still, she reasoned, it's one thing to find a fragrant flower; getting the smell into a bottle demanded genuine brilliance.

Tucka opened the perfume box. Inside was a crystal bottle topped with a crystal rose. She unstoppered it. She dipped a strip of paper in the amber liquid, waved it about for a few seconds to dry, raised it to her nose, and snuffled. She expected to be deeply disappointed; instead, she was devastated. Reezor had done the impossible. He had captured the scent of the *Rosa fragrantissima* and created the perfect perfume.

Tucka turned in her chair and gazed out the window over the city of Pinchester as she had thousands of times before. To Tucka's eye Pinchester looked like a shop window loaded with delicious treats — cakes and cookies and pastries — and across each of them was her name, boldly written in buttercream icing. The city was hers, and the sight of it never failed to stir her imagination. But today something was different. The view had subtly changed. Tucka brooded, and as she brooded, she proceeded one by one to pull the petals from every rose in the bouquet.

"She loves him. She loves him not," she chanted. "She loves him. She loves him not."

By the time she finished, the floor was littered with petals, and she had reached a decision. She did not love Reezor Bleesom. In fact, she hated him. And she intended to put him out of business.

Tucka buzzed Clareen. "Call housekeeping up here. These

roses don't hold up at all. And cancel all my appointments for the next few days. I've got a project that can't wait."

"But your five o'clock appointment is already here. Dr. Wollar is downstairs in the lobby."

"Dr. Wollar? I don't know any Wollar!"

"You hired him."

"And just why did I hire a doctor?"

"You hired him to run your new lab right after that scandal at Reezor Bleesom! Remember? He was a troublemaker."

"You bet he was!" said Tucka. Now she remembered him. "Send him right up!"

Chapter 3
SAVED BY THE BELL

Postmouse Lista Blenwipple had been gone barely a minute when the shop door opened again.

"Forget something?" Hermux asked.

But it was not Lista who breezed into the shop whistling a cheerful tune. It was Hermux's fiancée, Linka Perflinger.

"I've got good news!" she said. Linka was the type of mouse that most people describe as vivacious. She was forceful and direct. And that day she looked particularly forceful in her khaki flight uniform with hot pink piping. Normally Hermux would have been very glad to have Linka drop in unexpectedly. However, today she had come to pick up the guest list for the wedding. And now, thanks to Lista, the list was a shambles. He would have to start all over again. He tried for a happy, natural smile. It was a big smile. He could feel the air on his back teeth.

He didn't fool Linka for one second.

"What's wrong, sweetie?" she asked. "Did something happen?"

"It's not important," said Hermux. "What's your news?" He did his best to sound excited and interested.

"I think I found a dress. It's at a little shop on Glimcody Lane. I'm meeting Beulith there in half an hour to show her."

At the sound of Beulith's name, Nip put his paper down. He was sweet on their friend Beulith Varmint. "You want me to come along?" he asked.

"Nope. Girls only," said Linka firmly. "You'll just get bored and irritate us. If you want to see her, why don't you meet her afterward and take her to dinner? In fact, why don't we all go to dinner?"

"Let's do it!" said Nip. He licked the last of the cream filling from his fingers. "I'm already hungry. What time?"

"Hermux?" asked Linka. "Is that all right?"

Hermux hesitated. "I'm not sure. I may have to work this evening."

"Work? Oh no. I'm sorry!" Linka looked so concerned. It broke Hermux's heart.

He held up the guest list. "I have to finish this."

Linka's look of concern faded. She began to drum her nails on the counter. To Hermux this was not a good sign. He and Linka had been through some fur-raising adventures together. They had survived bullets, bombs, even cases of dynamite. In hindsight, being tied to a case of dynamite had been easier than enduring the look of disappointment in Linka's eyes.

"Hermux, you promised!" she said. "We can't do anything until we know how many people are coming. We're running out of time!" She opened her shoulder bag and got out her *Happily Ever After Wedding Planner*. "Now I've to got to push the entire schedule back a whole day."

"Maybe I should leave," Nip offered. "I could run over to Lanayda's and get coffee. You want some?"

"No, thanks," said Linka distractedly.

15

"I think I'll go anyway. It's time for Lanayda to mark down the day-old donuts."

"Well?" Linka asked Hermux when Nip was gone. "Do I get an explanation?"

As though in answer to Hermux's prayers, the telephone rang.

"Excuse me," he said. He lifted the receiver. "Hello. Hermux Tantamoq Watchmaker. Hermux speaking." He paused a moment and listened. His eyes widened. "Who?" He spoke as though he didn't believe his ears. "Could you repeat that?"

"Who is it?" Linka whispered.

Hermux shook his head at Linka. "I see," he said. "Yes. Of course I do."

"Is it the caterer?" Linka asked helpfully. "I gave him this number. Tell him I'll call him back."

"Sssshh!" hissed Hermux. "I can't hear!"

"I said, 'Is that the caterer?' "

"No!" Hermux answered, a little too loudly. There was a sharp sound from the phone. Hermux turned away from Linka. "No. I'm sorry," he apologized. "Not you! I was talking to someone here in the shop." He covered the phone. "It's somebody important!" he told Linka.

"Who?"

Hermux uncovered the phone. "Could you hold on for just a moment, please? I've got a small emergency in the shop. I'll be right back." He laid the receiver down gently, gathered up Nip's newspaper, and motioned Linka to follow him back to the workshop.

Hermux handed Linka the paper and pointed to the article on the front page. "It's Androse DeRosenquill!" he whispered. "He's got a huge job restoring a historic clocktower in Thorny

End. And we could really use the money, if you know what I mean!"

Hermux rushed back to the phone. "All taken care of," he said. He grabbed his notepad. "Now, how can I help you?"

"I have a project for you." Androse DeRosenquill's voice crackled with impatience. "And I want you to get started right away."

"Sounds wonderful!" said Hermux. He started doodling dollar signs. "And when would you like to get together to discuss it?"

"Tomorrow morning. I've wasted far too much time already."

Hermux added smiley faces to the dollar signs. "Tomorrow morning would be perfect. I'll clear my schedule. What time should I expect you here?"

"Expect me *there*?" Androse DeRosenquill snorted in disbelief. "At your shop? In Pinchester? That's very funny, Mr. Tantamoq. But I certainly hope your work is sharper than your wit. If you want the job, you'll be here at nine A.M. tomorrow morning."

"Where is 'here'?" Hermux asked uncertainly.

"Thorny End, Mr. Tantamoq. Do you need a geography lesson too? Nine A.M. on the dot. I don't trust people who are late."

There was no way Hermux could get there on time. From Pinchester it was a three-hour drive at least. Besides, he didn't own a car. He didn't even drive. But before he could explain, DeRosenquill hung up.

Hermux was still listening to the dial tone when Linka emerged from the workshop. He put down the phone.

Linka threw her arms around him and squeezed him. "I'm so

17

proud of you!" she said. "It sounds like a very important job."

"It is," Hermux said miserably.

Linka stepped back. "You don't sound excited. What's wrong?"

"I'm not going to get the job."

"Why not?"

"Because he wants me in Thorny End tomorrow morning at nine. Otherwise, no job."

"Is that all?" Linka asked cheerfully. "Why didn't you say so?"

"I just did!" Sometimes Linka's cheerfulness could be exasperating.

"I'll fly you down first thing in the morning. That's what I wanted to tell you. I'm taking tomorrow off to fly around and look at country inns. Beulith thinks a country inn wedding would be very romantic. There's a famous inn in Thorny End. You can check it out when you're finished with your meeting. That will save me some time. We'll get an early start, and I'll pick you up tomorrow night on the way back."

It was at moments like this that Hermux remembered why he loved Linka so much. Linka Perflinger was not your typical young mouse. She had her own airplane, and she loved to fly. Adventure was her profession. It was plain silly to let himself get so worked up about overdue guest lists and over-budget budgets. Together he and Linka would figure these things out. After all, they were just problems. Getting married was an adventure like any other.

"Only better," thought Hermux.

Chapter 4
THE JOKER IS WILD

Killium Wollar might have been a nice-looking mouse if it weren't for his appearance. And he might have been a likable mouse if it weren't for his personality. He was just too smart for his own good. Or anyone else's.

His first-grade teacher told him he was a genius. Killium shared her opinion. She also told him that geniuses were expected to work hard. "Nonsense," thought Killium. Hard work was for dumb kids. They didn't have much choice. He did.

He never studied, but he managed to ace every test. He never did homework unless it was about something he liked. He liked spiders, snakes, poisons of any kind, bacteria (especially vicious flesh-eating varieties), bombs, bullets, parasites, medieval instruments of torture, and all kinds of practical jokes. He didn't like poetry or history or stories about brave little mice and courageous young squirrels. In his book they were all chumps. And Killium was no chump.

Eventually he grew up. School came to an end. There were no more tests to ace. No more homework to avoid. He stayed home all day and listened to music and raided the refrigerator. Then one day Killium's father gave him some very bad news.

"It's time for you to get a job."

"I don't want one!" said Killium.

"You'll need one. It's also time for you to move out of the house."

Killium's mother had already packed his clothes.

It was against his principles, but Killium found a job. He got hired as a junior laboratory assistant at Reezor Bleesom Fragrances.

"Cool!" he thought. "Maybe I'll get to work on a stink bomb."

Instead, he got assigned to work on Reezor's latest pet project. Reezor wanted a new perfume that captured the spirit of youth. And he was offering a big prize—ten thousand dollars. Killium was impressed.

Reezor told his employees, "Just remember, youth is *innocent.* It's *irreverent.* It's *wild.* Young people are *REAL!* You've got two weeks. Have some fun with it!"

The time passed quickly. Everyone in the lab was caught up in a fever pitch of work. Everyone except Killium. He spent his time daydreaming about what he could buy with ten thousand dollars. The day of the contest dawned, and he still hadn't done a thing. Then minutes before Reezor arrived at the laboratory to pick the winner, Killium disappeared. He returned a few minutes later and placed a plain-looking bottle on the table with the other entries. Reezor breezed in, accompanied by a swarm of reporters and photographers.

Reezor was famous for his sensitive nose, and he put it right to work. The first entry was called Tender Heart. Reezor sniffed it. Then he proceeded to identify its ingredients. "Honeysuckle, lily of the valley, and pumpkin." As always he was right. "I like this one," he said. "It's innocent, all right. But I don't know if I'd actually call it irreverent."

The second entry was Toy Box. "Cedar and chocolate with overtones of peanut butter," he said. He was right again. "It's innocent. It's irreverent. But I'd say it's more charming than wild."

The third was Tantrum. "Peppermint. Mustard, bubble gum, and just a hint of skunk cabbage, I think. It's innocent. It's irreverent. And it's wild, all right." Reezor smiled. Then he sniffed again. "But real? I'm not sure bubble gum qualifies as real."

He moved on to Killium's bottle. "BLEESOM N°1," he read with a chuckle. "Now that has a nice ring to it, doesn't it?" He opened the bottle and let the smell waft up toward him. "This one's easy," he said. "Baby oil, for starts." He sniffed lightly. "And there's something else there. But I can't think what. It's familiar, though." He sniffed again. "Hmmmpf. It's certainly innocent. And it's got an irreverent quality I like." He sniffed again and wrinkled his nose. "And a definite wild side!" It was really beginning to grow on him. He took a deep whiff. "It's very real! Almost too real," he said. "I think this is it!" He held the bottle up for the photographers. "Ladies and gentlemen, we've got a winner! The Reezor Bleesom Spirit of Youth Prize goes to—" He read the label. "Killium Wollar. For BLEESOM N°1! Is Mr. Wollar here?"

Killium sauntered to the podium. "I don't have a speech," he told the crowd. "I guess I didn't really expect to win. It was kind of a joke."

"Well, this is no joke!" Reezor presented Killium a check for ten thousand dollars. "But you've got to tell me what's in it. I'm seldom stumped."

"It's baby oil, like you said."

"But there's something else, isn't there? I know that smell. It's very familiar, but I can't quite put my finger on it."

Killium smirked. "Oh, you don't want to put your finger on it!"

"Let me be the judge of that," said Reezor. He made a big show of splashing on some BLEESOM Nº1 while the photographers took pictures. "Tell me what it is!"

"Okay," said Killium. "But it's just what it says—number one. I found an old bottle of baby oil, and I peed in it. You wanted a young smell. I can't think of anything that smells younger than a wet diaper. Can you?"

Reezor stopped smelling his wrist. He took back his check and fired Killium on the spot. The picture and the story made the paper that afternoon.

OUI! OUI! A NO-NO FOR REEZOR BLEESOM

When Tucka read it, she laughed so hard that she wet her own pants. The next day she offered Killium a job running her new lab.

"You're the joker," she told him. "I need new ideas. So surprise me! And don't think I shock as easily as Reezor. I've seen everything. I'll give you six months."

Today the six months were up. And as he stepped off the elevator, Killium didn't have much to show.

In her office Tucka waited impatiently for Dr. Killium Wollar. She couldn't remember much about him, but any mouse

22

with the good sense and technical know-how to humiliate Reezor Bleesom in public must be a fine scientist. Perhaps he had other admirable qualities as well. Wouldn't it be nice, for example, if he were handsome too? And sophisticated. And charming. And single. Tucka closed her eyes, and the scientist of her dreams took shape with astonishing speed. His smile was incandescent. He had thick, glossy fur with golden highlights. His eyes were burning pools of passion ringed with thick dark lashes. He wore a spotless white tailored linen lab coat. And he lived for one thing only—her. To protect the happiness of the woman he loved, he wouldn't hesitate to destroy anything that stood in her path. And that included Reezor Bleesom.

"Dr. Wollar to see you," Clareen announced.

Tucka opened her eyes and greeted Killium Wollar in the flesh. Unfortunately, he was no dream.

Chapter 5
LIP SERVICE

What Tucka wanted was a scientific knight in shining armor. What she got was a nerd in a sweatshirt, carrying a suitcase. But she was used to being disappointed by men. Hiril Mennus, Hinkum Stepfitchler III, Corpius Crounce. The list went on and on, but this was an all-time low. Killium had been there for a few minutes now, and Tucka was still too stunned to say a word. She felt like putting her head down on her desk and crying.

Killium found Tucka's strained silence unnerving. He began to whistle uncomfortably. He had a feeling he might be looking for a new job soon. That was probably just as well. Lately things hadn't been going well at the lab anyway. And that was putting it mildly.

"I've got one thing to show you," he said finally. He opened his suitcase and set a strange-looking device on Tucka's desk. He went on. "I've been experimenting with the effects of histamines on body tissues. I've discovered some funny things."

Tucka didn't want to listen, but once he had gotten started, Wollar wouldn't shut up. He droned on and on while she did her best to ignore him. Then a phrase penetrated her consciousness.

"I guess you could call it a cure for thin lips—"

"What did you say?" Tucka asked. She sat up and fixed her inquisitive eyes on him.

"I said I guess you could call it a cure for thin lips." Killium laughed uncomfortably. "If that sort of thing interested you."

"I'm interested." She was all attention now. "With this silly machine?"

Killium shrugged. Tucka pulled it toward her. She looked it over. It was a black box with a large tube set in the top. The tube ended in a mouthpiece.

"How does it work?"

"The subject places her lips against the mouthpiece, fastens the strap around her head, and pushes that red button—"

Before he could say another word, Tucka's lips were in place and her head was strapped in.

"I wouldn't—" Killium started to say.

But he was too late. Tucka had already jabbed the red button. The box began to vibrate. Tucka had received hundreds of exotic beauty treatments. And after the rough day she had had, she felt like she deserved a little pampering. She closed her eyes and pictured a cool herbal mist beginning to rise through the tube. Soon it would reach her lips and the soothing would begin. But what reached her was neither cool nor soothing. A blinding hot pain seared her lips. She tried to push the contraption away from her, but the strap held it tight.

She ripped the strap from her head and a huge, dying bee fell onto her desk. Tucka screamed bloody murder.

Clareen was there in an instant.

"So does that mean you don't like my Luscious Lip-Fix machine?" Killium asked.

"You're fired!" Tucka shrieked. She turned to Clareen. "Get security up here and throw this idiot out!"

The guards arrived moments later and roughly escorted Killium toward the elevators. Clareen stayed behind to comfort Tucka. "I love what you've done to your lips," she told her, trying to cheer her up.

"Really?" asked Tucka. She dried her tears and rushed to the mirror in her dressing room. She was amazed at what she saw. Her lips had puffed up like two jelly donuts. She tried a pout. It was a SUPER POUT.

"Stop!" she yelled to the guards. "Bring him back!"

They dragged Killium in and dropped him in front of her desk. He landed with a crash and collapsed on the floor like a wet sock puppet. Tucka looked down at him and smiled. It was a megawatt smile. "No need to rush off," she said. "Would you like a chair?" She pushed one toward him with her toe, then she addressed Clareen. "I think we'll move into the conference room. Why don't you make things comfortable for us?" To the guards she said simply, "And why don't you make yourselves scarce? Can't you see I'm in a meeting?"

Chapter 6
ON THE NOSE

Walking home that night, Hermux passed by Mrs. Thankton's Florist Shop. The window was filled with spring bouquets of violets and miniature daffodils. The sight of the flowers gave Hermux an idea. He would send Linka a bouquet. After all, they had almost had their first fight. And it had been his fault.

It was nearly closing time. Mrs. Thankton was busy at the counter with a customer, so Hermux looked around the shop and tried to decide what sort of bouquet Linka would like best. Mrs. Thankton was famous for her moss work. Her newest creation sat right inside the door. She had covered an entire tabletop with thick green moss and then planted it with a tiny forest of ferns. In the middle sat a little plaster hedgehog gnome on a real mushroom, smoking a pipe that puffed real smoke.

Hermux thought it was all very elegant. But he couldn't remember whether Linka liked gnomes or not. Then he noticed the towering arrangement that filled the center of the shop. It was made up of bamboo, banana leaves, big orange flowers like savage birds, and ten pineapples at least. It even had a tiki torch, although it wasn't lit.

"Ha!" thought Hermux. "I know she'd like that. It's probably expensive, but I don't care!"

The cash register shut with a loud bang, and Hermux heard Mrs. Thankton say very irritably, "There's your money back! Every penny of it!"

The customer muttered, "I'm really sorry. But what can I do? She insisted!"

"I know," said Mrs. Thankton wearily. "She always insists."

On her way out the young mouse avoided making eye contact with Hermux. She looked genuinely embarrassed.

"Look at this!" Mrs. Thankton said. She held up a bunch of bare rose stems. "*Rosa fragrantissima!* The best rose in the business. And Miss Mertslin claims that the petals fell off the minute she unwrapped the bouquet. One day I'm going to—" She stopped herself. She dropped the stems into the trash and just barely managed a smile. "It's good to see you, Hermux. You're one my nicest customers. What can I do for you this evening?"

Hermux pointed at the giant arrangement. "I want to buy that bouquet and have it delivered right away."

"I'm sorry, Hermux, I made that for the Tropikini Hotel."

"Oh," said Hermux, disappointed.

"What did you want it for?"

"I want to send it to Linka. We sort of had an argument—"

"Ah!" she said. "Your first fight. That's so romantic! But you know, that is probably not quite the right bouquet to send anyway. We might want to think about something a little more intimate." She clapped her hands enthusiastically. "I think I've got just the thing!"

She disappeared to the back of the shop and returned with a large bundle wrapped in brown paper.

"I just got these in. They're really rare. You're the first person I've shown them to. I've got a secret source." She unwrapped the flowers and watched Hermux for his reaction.

The roses were pale red. Hermux thought they looked a little plain.

"I guess they're pretty," he said. "Sort of."

"They may not look unusual, but smell them, Hermux! I've been selling roses my whole life, and this is the best-smelling rose ever. And that includes the *fragrantissima*. But don't tell that to Androse DeRosenquill."

Hermux leaned closer to the counter and gave a tentative sniff. "Nice," he thought. "They smell like honey." He touched the tip of his nose to the center of a flower and sniffed again, this time more deeply. Very nice. Honey with raspberries and spice. And something else. Something sweet and enticing. Hermux buried his face in the roses and breathed in deeply. His nostrils quivered with pleasure. His sinuses reverberated. An explosion of memories went off deep in his brain. He remembered apple orchards in April. Honeysuckle summers. The sharpness of lemons. And then something even sharper than lemons. Something too strong to call pleasure. It felt more like having stuck his nose into an electric socket. And it felt more and more like someone was turning up the juice. Hermux couldn't take it anymore.

He jerked upright and squealed, "Owwww!"

"Oh, dear," said Mrs. Thankton. "I hope you didn't get a thorn!"

But it was no thorn. Attached to the tip of Hermux's nose was an enormous bee, buzzing angrily and pulsing its body as it pumped the last of its venom into his nose.

Mrs. Thankton was astonished.

Hermux pulled the bee from his nose. He looked around the

29

shop desperately. He grabbed a bucket of daisies. He dumped them on the floor and plunged his entire head into the bucket of cold water.

"Ahhh!" he gurgled. The shock of the cold nearly canceled out the sizzling sting of the bee. After a minute he raised his head. Mrs. Thankton examined his nose with horror. It had turned fire engine red and begun to swell ominously.

"Oh, dear," she said again. "I think you'd better soak awhile longer."

Hermux took a breath and dunked his nose. Before long he began to shiver.

"I'll go get you some ice," Mrs. Thankton told him. "That should help with the swelling."

Ten minutes later Hermux was sitting on a stool at the counter. He had a towel around his neck and a white gauze bandage around his nose.

"This has never happened before!" Mrs. Thankton assured him. "I'm so sorry! I don't know what to say."

"Inth nahnt yohr fahnt," murmured Hermux. "Int wahn an anntident." Hermux blew his nose delicately. "It could have happened to anyone."

"Well, I'm sorry it happened to you, Hermux. Do you still want to send them to Linka? I understand if you don't."

"Do you think they're safe?" he asked.

"I just examined the other roses carefully. There was only one bee. And he's dead. I mean 'she.' " Mrs. Thankton held out a paw and showed Hermux the body of the bee.

Hermux took it from her gingerly. "My goodness. It's big, isn't it?"

"I would say extremely big."

Hermux turned it over. Its abdomen showed curious markings. Hermux removed his magnifying loupe from his vest pocket. He opened it and fixed the lens to his eye. He held the bee close and examined it. The fur on the bee's belly seemed to grow in a distinct pattern. To Hermux it looked as though two letters were spelled out in golden hairs amongst the black. He squinted for better focus. They definitely appeared to be letters. "An I," he thought. "And an M." He showed them to Mrs. Thankton.

"How peculiar," he said. "What do you think that means?"

"I have no idea. Do you suppose it could be some sort of message?"

Chapter 7
IN THE MOOD

Tucka's conference room was designed for comfort. She had changed into more comfortable clothes for the evening and lit the fireplace and candles. She did her best thinking by candlelight, and what she was thinking now was that it was a shame that Killium looked like such a loser. Otherwise he had the potential to be a lot of fun. He seemed to be every bit as wicked as she was. And almost as smart. The question was: could she ever get past his scrawny body, bad grooming, and lousy taste in clothes? She decided that the answer, like so many of the important things in life, depended finally on bone structure. She would have to maneuver him into a good light and look him over carefully. In the meantime there were other questions to consider. The Luscious Lip-Fix device rested on the coffee table before them.

"I call them Killer Bees," Killium told her.

"Killer!" said Tucka. "How sweet!"

She poured them each another glass of Fizzy Bitters '96. "To Tucka's Luscious Lip-Fix!" She sipped carefully. Against the cool surface of the glass her lips felt as plump and luscious as overripe peaches. They also hurt like blazes. "Oh, well," she thought. "No pain, no gain." She leaned back into the cushy couch, extended her toes toward the fire, and practiced smiling lusciously.

"Tell me again how it works," she said.

Killium explained how bee stings worked. He found himself in a very odd situation. He couldn't figure Tucka out. One minute she was having him tossed out on his ear. The next minute they were sipping Fizzy Bitters by the fire. This part was certainly fun, but he couldn't shake the uncomfortable feeling that Tucka might be setting him up for an even bigger fall.

"Couldn't someone just use their own bees?" Tucka asked.

"Nope. Mine are better. They're genetically modified. Normal bees aren't as aggressive, and their sting isn't powerful enough. The swelling wouldn't last."

"And just how long does the swelling last?"

"About two days."

Tucka did some quick calculations. "That would be one hundred eighty Luscious Lip-Fix treatments per customer per year, give or take a few days off for holidays, et cetera. Say we charged five dollars per treatment—that works out to be nine hundred dollars per customer per year. Not bad." She smacked her luscious lips at the thought. "Ouch!" she said.

"Of course, there could be a downside."

"Oh?" said Tucka. She hated downsides. "What?"

"The treatments might become addictive."

Tucka chortled. "Honey, in this business, addiction is not considered a downside. It's the whole point."

Killium laughed. "Want to see something cool?" he asked.

"Sure."

Killium turned the Luscious Lip-Fix over and dumped the

33

bee out on the table. By now it was completely dead. He flipped it onto its back. "See that? On its stomach?"

Tucka focused a magnifying glass on the bee's stomach. "Poor thing," she thought. It really was beautiful.

"There?" she asked. "The gold marks?"

"Can you read them?"

Tucka's heart quickened. Yes! She could read them. There in the bee's fur was her company logo.

"Aren't you clever?" Tucka said. "You even got the trademark."

"A little extra bonus," said Killium. He was feeling positively suave.

Tucka traced the outline of her monogram with a long, elegant claw. "My little Killer Bee," she sighed. "You're going to make me a fortune!"

Tucka looked up at Killium. As she did, the fire blazed suddenly, illuminating his face in highlight and shadow. There might be some good bone structure there after all.

Killium caught her smiling. "What?" he asked.

"You know, you're kind of cute."

"I am?" He had always thought so, but Tucka was the first person to agree with him. She must be even smarter than he thought.

"You've got good bone structure. You could take more advantage of it."

"I could? How?"

"It would take me too long to list everything," she said. "I'll put a few things together."

"Like what?"

"For starts maybe a little grooming kit."

"To bring out the animal in me?"

"Something like that."

Killium winked at her and shook his head devilishly, dislodging a cloud of dandruff. Tucka gracefully moved her glass out of its path.

"Maybe a new haircut and some new clothes," she said. "I could see you in a more executive look."

"I'm executive material for sure. So you can see that, can't you?"

"Oh, I can see right through you, Killium. You're a regular little diamond in the rough. But in the meantime let's get back to those bees." In her mind Tucka pictured herself behind the wheel of a bee-powered steamroller headed right for Reezor Bleesom. Once her Luscious Lip-Fix went on sale, it would be time for *him* to smell the roses. And weep! She couldn't wait! "How long will it take you to go into production?"

"A few months," he said.

"That's too long! I need something right now. And I need something big. What else are you working on?"

"Nothing much."

"Then what have you been doing for the last six months?"

Tucka watched as Killium considered his answer. She could tell he had been up to something. She slid closer on the couch. She stretched her tail languorously and draped it along the back of the couch. "Tell me," she purred. She tickled one of his ears with the tip of her tail. "I want to know all about it."

Killium looked at her.

"You know you want to tell me," Tucka said. She poured him another glass of Fizzy Bitters, then prodded him with a slipper-clad foot. "Tell Mama everything."

"All right," he said. "But don't get mad."

"With these lips?" She gave him her SUPER POUT. "How could I get mad at you?"

"Well," Killium began, "I've been conducting some experiments with plants."

"What kind of experiments?"

"I've been killing roses."

"You've been killing roses! That's what I'm paying you for? Why would anybody kill roses?"

"You said you wouldn't get mad!" Killium reminded her.

"All right. All right." Tucka calmed herself. "And pray tell, why have you been killing roses?"

"I've been practicing."

"Why didn't I think of that?" she asked. "And exactly what are you practicing for?"

"Reezor Bleesom's been planting this fantasy garden, see? He's spent a whole fortune on roses. And I figure he owes me big-time, so one night I thought I might just sneak over there and kill me about ten thousand dollars' worth of roses. You know I won that ten thousand dollars from him fair and square, and he's going to pay one way or another!"

Tucka's jaw dropped.

"You're mad, aren't you?" Killium accused angrily.

"On the contrary, my dear! I'm not mad. You're the one who's mad. Stark raving!"

"Am I fired then?" He started to get up.

"Fired?" Tucka cackled. "Of course you're not fired! I'm giving you a promotion! I'm making you vice president of extermination. And have you had any luck with your rose-killing?"

"I'm getting close."

"Well, get closer! Reezor's big party is on Saturday. And I want it ruined. Surprise me with something!"

Chapter 8
A QUIET EVENING AT HOME

"I'm home!" Hermux called. He went straight to his study to check on Terfle.

Terfle waved from her cage. She was so excited to show Hermux what she had done that day that she didn't notice his bandaged nose. Since she had gone to work at the Varmint Theater, Terfle had blossomed artistically. In addition to assisting in the costume department, Hermux's artist friend Mirrin Stentrill had encouraged Terfle to try her hand at drawing. The results had been very promising. Now Terfle was studying with Mirrin one afternoon a week at her art studio and spending most of her free time drawing.

"New work?" Hermux asked.

Terfle pushed her tiny sketchbook toward the door. Hermux picked it up carefully. He got out his magnifying loupe and began to study each page one at a time. It was only then that Terfle realized that something terrible had happened to his nose.

"They're quite good!" Hermux said, handing her back the sketchbook. "You should be very, very proud. I especially like the portrait of Linka. I'd like to get that one blown up, if you don't mind."

Terfle nodded. She pointed at his nose and cocked her head questioningly.

"Oh, this?" Hermux said. "It's nothing. I'll tell you all about it after we eat."

While Hermux prepared dinner for both of them, Terfle organized her art supplies and stowed them in her satchel so she would be ready to work when she got to the theater the next morning. Glissin, the costume mistress, was going to do fittings for the chorus squirrels' new dresses, and Terfle planned to draw them in action. It would be a real challenge for her technically, but both Glissin and Mirrin thought she was ready for it.

Terfle was a ladybug. Technically she was Hermux's pet ladybug. But since she had collaborated with him on his most recent adventure, she thought of herself more as his professional associate. And she encouraged him to do the same.

Hermux was happy to do so. After all, Terfle was much more than just a pet. And she always had been. She was his confidante and his advisor in matters of the heart and in the fine points of style and fashion. Terfle had very definite ideas about style, and she was blessed with good taste.

After they finished dinner and Hermux had told the story of the bee sting, he asked, "Do you think you could help me with the wedding guest list? I'm having a hard time making decisions. And this nose isn't helping." He felt a sharp twinge and reached for the ice pack.

Terfle clicked her wings sympathetically and got out a pencil.

Hermux laid the list out on his desk. Terfle started at the top and worked her way down, pausing at each name long enough for Hermux to read it out loud. When she made her decision, she made a check mark or an X besides the name. She was generous but firm in her recommendations. Friends should be invited. Friends of friends should not. Relatives on speaking terms should be invited. But family feuds would be respected. That eliminated more than a dozen people on Hermux's mother's side alone. An hour later, the list was done. When he read the list over again, Hermux realized that the wedding could actually be fun.

"Thank you," said Hermux. "I should have asked you to begin with."

Terfle nodded in agreement. Then she yawned.

"You're right. We should get to bed. You've got to be at the theater early, and I've got to meet Linka at the airport first thing."

Hermux brushed his teeth, combed his fur, and put on his pajamas. Then he got into bed and opened his journal. "I'm not sure where to start," he said. It had been an unusual day. He thought back through it.

Thank you for marriage. And for budgets and lists. Thank you for Terfle's talent and for small-scale art supplies. Thank you for clocktowers and repair jobs and wild roses.

He paused a moment. He touched one finger lightly to his nose. It throbbed painfully. Nevertheless, he wrote:

And thank you for bees. I'm sorry that bee stung me. And I'm sorry it had to die.

The next day dawned clear and calm in Pinchester. It was a fine day for flying. After takeoff Linka set her course south-southeast.

"I called my friend who grew up in Thorny End last night," Linka told Hermux. "I asked her about the DeRosenquills, and I got an earful."

"About what?" asked Hermux.

"Well, the clocktower for one. And Androse DeRosenquill. And the Jeckels."

"What are jeckels?"

"Not what. Who. There used to be two big families in the rose business, the Jeckels and the DeRosenquills. They were bitter rivals. Eventually the DeRosenquills drove the Jeckels out of business. All the Jeckels held on to was the family mansion and a little island out in the bay. Then the DeRosenquills' son married the Jeckels' daughter, and he ended up with everything. That was Androse DeRosenquill. Villa DeRosenquill used to be called Jeckel House."

"And I suppose the DeRosenquills lived happily ever after?"

41

"Not quite," said Linka. "And that's quite a story."

But she didn't get to tell it. They were approaching the fertile valley of the Paddlepick River, and it was time to begin their descent. Below them the terraced hillsides appeared to be quilted in roses. Rows of red roses. Yellow roses. Pink, coral, lavender, and white. Long-stemmed. Climbing. Roses for planting in gardens. Roses for making bouquets and corsages. Roses for birthdays. Roses for romance.

Hermux pressed his nose against the window for a better view and to enjoy the feel of the cold glass on his sore nose. "It's very beautiful," he said.

"Not as beautiful as these," said Linka. She had put a few of Hermux's roses in the bud vase on the control panel. Their perfume filled the cabin. "That was awfully sweet of you, Hermux. I'm sorry I got cranky."

"It's okay," he said. He rubbed his nose gently. "Maybe I should take my bandage off now."

"You might want to," said Linka. "You do look a little odd."

"How's this?" He showed off his new slightly lumpy profile.

"I think the swelling is going down." Linka tried to sound reassuring. "Now, you're sure you won't forget about the inn? When you're done with Mr. DeRosenquill, go out there and take a look. It used to be very nice, but I haven't seen it in years. Make sure you find out what dates they have available this fall. Find out how many guest rooms they have. Try the food. And take a look at the kitchen—make sure it's clean! At least in Thorny End we wouldn't have to worry about flowers. I'll see if I can make it to all four inns on my list. And we can compare notes when I pick you up tonight. Then we can decide."

Despite Linka's smooth landing, Hermux felt a little dizzy as the plane taxied toward the terminal. "Could be the loss of altitude," he told himself. "Or the flowers, maybe. Or the wedding."

Chapter 10
THE SUITE LIFE

Killium sat up with a start. He was in a hotel room. A very nice hotel room. Details of the night before were starting to come back to him. Tucka's assistant, Clareen, had booked him into an executive suite at the Pinchester Arms Hotel, courtesy of Tucka Mertslin Cosmetics.

He clicked on the reading lamp and a remarkable sight met his eyes. There on the bedside table, propped up where he would see it as soon as he woke, was Tucka's check. It was made out for twenty-five thousand dollars. And it was made out to him. It was not a dream. Tucka had written him the check as a bonus for the Luscious Lip-Fix. And she had promised him another one just like it if he ruined Reezor's big party on Saturday.

Killium stood up on the mattress and bounced until he was able to touch the ceiling. "I'm rich!" he shouted. "I'm rich!" He flopped down on his back and cradled the check next to his heart. After a while he realized that all the exercise had made him hungry.

He drew the curtains and called room service.

"I want breakfast sent right up. I want a cheesy-cheese omelette, blueberry waffles, mapleseed pancakes, plenty of syrup, fresh cherry juice, and a pot of coffee." It was fun to give orders. "And send me the morning paper! I didn't even have a chance to read it yesterday!"

As soon as he hung up, the doorbell rang.

"Nice service!" he said.

But it was not room service. It was a bellboy who carried in a stack of boxes from Orsik & Arrbale.

"This came with the packages," he told Killium. He handed Killium a note.

Dear Killium,

Here's a start on your new executive look. I also put in a few things from my Crude Dude line. Start with the shampoo.

I will be down on Saturday for the party, and I expect a wonderful surprise to be waiting for me!

Tucka

Half an hour later Killium emerged from the bathroom. He looked like a new mouse from his glossy fur to his three-button suit. It was then that room service arrived.

Killium seated himself at the breakfast cart and poured himself a cup of coffee. He reached for the paper, and the phone rang. As he answered, he caught his reflection in the mirror on the wall. He was the very picture of an executive mouse. He already felt more important.

"Hello," he said. "Dr. Killium Wollar speaking."

It was Tucka calling on her private line. "I was so excited about our little project that I hardly slept a wink," she gushed. "Did the packages come?"

"Yeah."

"And?"

"I opened them."

"And?"

"The stuff's all right."

"All right?"

"Yeah."

"That's all I get for three handmade suits? Do you have any idea what those cost?"

"No," Killium said meekly.

"Plenty. So, what do you say?"

"Thank you?"

"That's better. Did you try the shampoo?"

"Yes."

"And?"

"Thank you," he said.

"You already said that. Did it work?"

"Smells nice."

"The dandruff, Killium. Did it stop the dandruff?"

Tucka was beginning to sound just like his mother. Killium sipped some coffee and tried to ignore her.

"I ordered you a home gymnasium," Tucka went on with enthusiasm. "It's got everything. I had it sent directly to the lab. Next week I'm sending my personal trainer down to get you up and running. We'll have you in shape in no time."

Killium opened the paper.

Tucka kept right on talking. Blah, blah, blah. But Killium had stopped listening. His eyes were riveted on the morning's headline:

"How did it end up on the beach?" he gasped.

"How did what end up on the beach?"

"Nothing!" Killium coughed. "What I said was, 'It's so nice that fitness is within reach.'"

"Well of course it's nice. But not everybody can afford it!"

"Listen," said Killium. "I gotta go now."

"Go? I'm not finished yet."

"Right," said Killium. "But Reezor's party is coming right up, and I've got stuff to do. I don't want to disappoint you."

"You don't?" Tucka's voice softened. "How touching!"

Killium fondled Tucka's check. "Yeah. It is, isn't it?"

Chapter 11
DARK SHADOWS

Hermux walked up the brick steps to the grand front terrace of the grand Villa DeRosenquill. He rang the bell firmly and waited.

A heavyset squirrel in a slightly threadbare butler's uniform scowled down at Hermux.

"We're not hiring," he said as though Hermux had already wasted too much of his time. "This is not the office even if we were hiring. And if we were, we wouldn't hire you. We don't hire mice. You need stamina to pick roses. No offense."

"No offense taken," Hermux said, trying to sound pleasant. He was, in fact, extremely offended. Hermux was a very hardworking mouse, and he had plenty of stamina. He had been known to stay up all night to repair particularly intricate and difficult clocks. He threw back his shoulders and drew himself up to his full height, which was still a good head shorter than the squirrel. "But you see, I'm not here about a job. I mean actually I am. But a different job. I've got an appointment with Androse DeRosenquill."

"He didn't mention it to me." The butler leaned forward toward Hermux and stared curiously at his nose. As butlers went, he wasn't very polite.

"Bee sting," said Hermux.

"Must have been a pretty big bee."

"It was." Hermux offered his business card. "My appointment is for nine o'clock."

"Watchmaker, huh? Seems like you'd be on time."

Hermux checked his watch. "I'm five minutes early."

"Five minutes is five minutes." Then he shrugged and motioned Hermux inside. "I'll tell Mr. DeRosenquill you're here. He's a stickler for schedules, though. You may have to wait."

When he was gone, Hermux took a look around. To the left of the entry hall was a cavernous living room in which the drapes were drawn. A single candle burned on the mantel of the massive fireplace. Above it hung an enormous photograph framed in gold and draped in black. Hermux tiptoed in and approached the picture.

It was a portrait of a young squirrel with prominent front teeth, sitting on the hood of a shiny red sports convertible. He wore driving gloves, sunglasses pushed up above the rusty gold fur of his forehead, and a racing jacket that said TEAM DEROSEN-QUILL & SON. He couldn't have been much more than twenty years old. A magnificent black-tipped brush of a tail bobbed above his head like a question mark, and in the candlelight his eyes seemed to flicker with amusement, as though the world was some sort of private joke.

"Buddlin DeRosenquill." The butler's voice, from the doorway, startled Hermux. "It was taken just two weeks before the accident."

49

"I didn't mean to snoop," Hermux apologized.

"Indeed," said the butler. "You were only having a look around."

"The candle caught my eye."

"It was intended to. Mr. DeRosenquill maintains this room as a memorial to his son."

Hermux rejoined the butler in the entry hall.

"I'm sorry. Were you terribly fond of him?"

"Me?" Hermux's question caught the butler off guard. "No. I can't say that I was. Buddlin DeRosenquill was a spoiled, irresponsible child. He caused me no end of trouble."

An uncomfortable silence fell over them.

"I'll take you back to the greenhouse now. Mr. DeRosenquill is working this morning."

He walked away stiffly, and Hermux followed. A long hallway led back through the gloomy house to a double door. It opened into a glassed-in walkway that connected to a large greenhouse. After the darkness of the house, Hermux found himself nearly blinded by the light. Inside the green-house the air was heavy with humidity and laden with the scent of roses.

"Mr. DeRosenquill is in the back," the butler told him. He turned and left.

Except for the sound of snipping, the greenhouse was si-lent. A narrow gravel path divided the space, and on either side of the path in perfectly tended raised beds towered the biggest rosebushes that Hermux had ever seen, covered with flowers the size of saucers. Hermux wished that Terfle were there to see them. She was a great lover of roses. Of course, for Terfle that was due, in large part, to the fact that aphids were also great lovers of roses. Hermux thought it unlikely that many aphids got the opportunity to visit the roses in Androse DeRosenquill's private greenhouse. But he still thought that Terfle would find the sight inspiring.

Chapter 12
CODE RED

Before driving back to Thorny End, Killium had an appointment to keep. He parked his van on a side street in downtown Pinchester and waited. On the van's side in faded letters it said:

THE INSTITUTE FOR POSITIVE THINKING

Back in the day, the institute had been very successful. It had its own island, its own ferry, plus buildings including guest cabins, a greenhouse, and a barn. But in recent years it had fallen on hard times. Positive Thinking wasn't what it used to be. When Tucka heard that the institute was for sale at a ridiculously low price, she couldn't resist. She wasn't sure what she would do with it. But she loved bargains. Besides, the institute was a very special place for Tucka Mertslin. It had changed her life.

As a young woman Tucka had gone to the island for a week-long Positive Thinking retreat. While she was there, she did group therapy. She fasted for hours at a time. She walked on hot coals wearing nothing but sandals. After a week of intensive training, she became a Positive Thinker. And what she thought about was getting rich. The experience taught her three important lessons.

- Wealth is the key to happiness.
- People are the key to wealth.
- Envy is the key to people.

The lessons had worked for her, and she had a corporate empire to prove it. Now she had her very own institute. In fact, it was her very own *secret* institute because, besides her lawyers, only Clareen and Killium knew about it.

The institute came with two employees, local squirrels named Hanger and Skuhl. They had both grown up in Thorny End and worked in the rose fields until the institute had opened. They did odd jobs around the place, and on occasion they served as night watchmen. Since Killium's arrival at the institute there hadn't been much to watch. Or many odd jobs for them to do. Until very recently.

Just that morning Hanger had taken the bus from Thorny End to Pinchester on a mysterious errand for Killium. Now Killium was supposed to pick him up and drive him back.

A chunky squirrel approached the van and tapped on the window.

"Hanger!" said Killium. "Let's go! Get a move on!"

Hanger climbed in. Killium started the van and pulled out into traffic.

"How did it go?" asked Killium.

"Fine, I guess," said Hanger.

"You did everything I told you?"

"Pretty much."

"People saw you?"

"Plenty of people."

"And the clothes?"

"They're right here." Hanger held out a shopping bag.

"You dope!" said Killium. "I told you to throw them away."

"No, you didn't! And don't snap at me, boss. You said I was doing you a big favor."

"Sorry! My mistake. I'll take care of it later. Any trouble with the police?"

"Nope. They even bought my ticket. Just like you said."

"Like clockwork," said Killium.

"What was that all about anyway?" Hanger asked.

Killium chuckled. "I was just playing a joke on an old buddy of mine."

Hanger scratched his head. "I guess I don't see what's so funny about a guy on a bus."

"It's kind of hard to explain," Killium said.

"So what's up with the suit?"

"Slick, huh? I got a big promotion," Killium bragged. "Vice president!"

"Good for you!" Hanger said. "So what does that make me?"

Killium thought about it.

"I'm giving you a promotion too," he said.

"You are?"

"I'm putting you in charge of security."

"Do I get a uniform?"

"Sure. Take your pick."

"What about Skuhl?"

"He reports to you."

"Sweet!" Hanger rubbed his hands together.

"And from now on, nobody comes near the institute. We're going top secret. You see anybody on the island, you've got orders to shoot."

"I don't have a gun."

"Then it's time you got one. Get one for Skuhl too."

Chapter 13

CUT SHORT

As Hermux followed the gravel path that led toward the center of the greenhouse, the sound of snipping grew louder. It was crisp and methodical, like the sound of a barber at work. Hermux emerged into a large, open area dominated by a worktable covered with rosebushes in big plastic pots. A squirrel sat with his back to Hermux, nearly obscured by the puffy tail hunched over his head. Before him a potted rose stood on a turntable. He turned it slowly, and as he examined the bush, he snipped.

"Mr. DeRosenquill?" Hermux asked.

The squirrel turned where he sat. "Mr. Tantamoq! Nice of you to come." He extended his free hand to Hermux, but he did not get up. He was seated in a wheelchair.

Hermux reached down and shook hands.

"What happened to your nose?" DeRosenquill asked.

"Bee sting," said Hermux.

"Must have been a heck of a bee!"

"It was."

"Must have hurt too!"

"It did."

"I wish I could have seen it!" DeRosenquill snickered. "Bring a chair around where I can see you."

Hermux fetched a metal chair and seated himself opposite DeRosenquill. He waited for DeRosenquill to speak.

Androse DeRosenquill was an elegant squirrel. His gray-streaked fur was impeccably groomed and clipped short, military style. He wore an expensive-looking dark suit that bore the DeRosenquill monogram stitched in gold. He appeared to be a squirrel who had led a pampered life. His nicked and scarred paws, however, told a different story.

Androse gave the rosebush a final turn and set it aside. "Are you familiar with the *Rosa fragrantissima*?" he asked.

Hermux nodded. "I've heard of it."

"The most perfect rose of all. And it's mine. I created it. Do you have any idea what it takes to create a rose?"

Hermux did not.

"Discipline, Mr. Tantamoq." He snipped a branch away from the rose. "You must prune out the weaklings. Are you a married mouse, Mr. Tantamoq?"

"No," said Hermux. "Not yet. But—"

"Then let me give you a piece of advice," Androse said. "Don't ever get married. And don't ever have children. I did both, and it's been nothing for me but misery and more misery." He snipped a branch. "But I had no choice. We are DeRosenquill and Son, Mr. Tantamoq. The greatest rose growers the world has ever known. And what does DeRosenquill and Son need in order to continue?" He snipped another branch. This one was larger than the last.

"I'm not sure," said Hermux. He began to wonder whether

coming to the Villa DeRosenquill had been such a good idea.

"DeRosenquill and Son needs a son, Mr. Tantamoq! A son!" He snipped a twig.

"I'm sorry for your loss," said Hermux sympathetically.

"Were you a disappointment to your father, Mr. Tantamoq?" He snipped again. The rose was decidedly lopsided now.

"I don't think so," said Hermux. He was beginning to feel sorry for the rose. "He wanted me to follow in his footsteps and I did. I became a watchmaker." Hermux hoped the conversation might turn now to the subject of the clocktower. He was anxious to know more about the plans for the restoration. But his answer only seemed to increase DeRosenquill's agitation.

"A father's footsteps! Is that too much to ask?" With three fierce snips he reduced the rose to a mere stump. He stared at it desolately. Then he hurled it across the table. It crashed to the ground and rolled to a stop. "I want you to find my son!"

Hermux was dumbfounded.

"I want you to find him and bring him back!"

"But I thought—" Hermux began. He began again. "I thought he was—"

"What, Mr. Tantamoq?" His eyes appeared slightly out of focus.

"I thought he was—dead." The word died on Hermux's lips.

DeRosenquill pushed violently back from the table. His chair coasted to a stop. "Dead? He's not dead. Even he wouldn't be that thoughtless! And you'll find him. You'll bring him back.

And you'll explain to him that DeRosenquill and Son has got to have a son. Got to! A son, Mr. Tantamoq! I don't care what it costs. It's already cost me everything." He set another rose on the turntable and began to snip. "Now leave me alone. Talk to Primm. I'm tired."

Chapter 14
O BROTHER, WHERE ART THOU?

Hermux opened the door and stepped out of the sunshine of the greenhouse and back into the gloom of the DeRosenquill house.

He had hardly taken ten steps when a door in the hallway popped open, causing Hermux to nearly leap out of his fur.

"There you are!" said a brusque voice. "I was coming to look for you!"

Silhouetted against the glare of the doorway stood an imposing squirrel.

Hermux was mute.

"Tarp told me you had an appointment with my father. What did you want with him?" The squirrel stepped out of the doorway and back into what looked like a very cluttered but comfortable office.

In the light Hermux was relieved to see a normal-enough-looking squirrel who was a bit older than him, perhaps in her thirties, he thought. She was dressed like a farmer in well-worn overalls. Her broad face was free of makeup, and she wore her fur pulled back in a simple bun.

"Primm DeRosenquill," she said, extending a hand.

Hermux extended his as well. "Uh . . . pleased to meet you. I'm Hermux Tantamoq."

"I know. Tarp told me. And you're a watchmaker?"

"Yes."

"And I suppose you're here to inquire about the contract for the clocktower."

"Yes," said Hermux. "At least I thought I was."

"I'm afraid you've wasted your time," she said, pleasantly but firmly. "When we're ready to accept bids for the work, we'll make an announcement. I'll keep your card on file. In the meantime I'm not sure how you managed to reach him, but I'll ask you not to contact my father again."

"But I didn't contact him," Hermux protested. "Your father contacted me. He asked me to come here this morning."

Hermux's explanation seemed to take her by surprise.

"I'm sure he was trying to be helpful. The clocktower project is very important to him," she replied. "But my father is not a well man."

"I got that impression."

"I see," she said. She arched her bushy eyebrows and studied Hermux a moment. "And what other impressions did you get?"

"He didn't really want to see me about the clocktower at all."

"No? What did he want to see you about?" She sounded suspicious.

Hermux wasn't sure how to put it. He decided to put it plainly. "Your father wanted to hire me to find your brother."

A sharp look of pain passed over Primm DeRosenquill's face.

"Of course," she said. "DeRosenquill and Son must have its son. At any cost!"

61

She turned away from Hermux and walked slowly to the desk that dominated the room. She sank down into the chair.

"Perhaps you'd better sit down too."

Hermux did as he was told. Primm put her elbows on the desk, then buried her face wearily in her hands. Primm's paws, like those of her father, were battered and scarred by rose thorns.

When she raised her head, he saw that she had been crying. She wiped her eyes. "I'm very tired, Mr. Tantamoq. It has not been a good year. First my brother's death. And now my father—what exactly did he say to you?"

Hermux tried to recall Androse's exact words. "First he asked me if I was a disappointment to my father. Then he said that your brother couldn't be dead because even he couldn't be that thoughtless. And that I was to find him and bring him back."

"Bring him back?"

"That's what he said."

"At any cost."

"Right," said Hermux. "He said that it had already cost him everything. He acted very odd. Is he having a nervous breakdown?" Hermux hoped that wasn't an impolite question. He didn't want to be impolite to Primm, especially because she had been very polite to him. She had noticed his swollen nose the minute he stepped into her office, but she still hadn't mentioned it.

"My father wouldn't be the first DeRosenquill to have a nervous breakdown," she said. "But let's hope not for now. What I don't understand is why my father would ask a watchmaker to find a missing son."

"Oh," said Hermux. "I think I can explain that. You see, besides being a watchmaker, I'm also a detective. I've worked on three cases. This would be my fourth. I mean, it would if your brother were still alive and he were missing."

"A watchmaking detective? That's very sweet." Primm smiled for the first time. She had the same prominent teeth he'd noticed on the portrait of her brother. She appeared to come to a decision. "Can I trust you, Mr. Tantamoq?" she asked.

"Please call me Hermux. And you can trust me. I'm very honest. You can ask my friends."

"All right, Hermux. I hope I won't regret this. I think I can explain now what my father meant by finding his son. You see, he had two sons. Besides Buddlin, I have or *had* an older brother named Plank. Plank had his own ideas about the life he wanted to live. He refused to become the son in DeRosenquill and Son. So Father disowned him. That was years ago, and Father has never spoken Plank's name again. After everything else that happened, he probably can't bring himself to say it."

"So maybe the old man is not crazy after all," thought Hermux. For the first time since he arrived at the Villa DeRosenquill, things were beginning to make at least a little sense. He said gently, "And perhaps now with your younger brother dead, your father would like to have his other son back?"

"You've got it, Hermux! It's DeRosenquill and *Son*, not DeRosenquill and Daughter," she answered with surprising bitterness. "A daughter won't do.

"I suppose it's not entirely his fault." Primm sighed and continued. "It's family tradition. Grandfather passed the business on to Father the same as his father before him. It was Father's duty to pass the business on to his son. When Plank didn't want it, Father tried to bully him into the business. And it backfired. With Buddlin he changed his approach. He tried spoiling him.

Buddlin got anything he wanted growing up. What he didn't want was work. At the end of the day, what does my father have? A missing son whose name he won't say, a dead playboy, and a smashed-up sports car. Luckily for DeRosenquill and Son, he's also got a dutiful daughter who stays here to clean up the messes that everyone else leaves behind."

Hermux listened intently.

"So now, Hermux, I guess it's up to you."

"I've never handled a missing-person case," said Hermux. "It sounds very interesting. How long has Plank been gone?"

Primm thought. "Nearly fifteen years."

Hermux gulped. "That's a long time."

"It seems like an eternity."

"What can you tell me about him?"

"Even as a little boy Plank had his own ideas. And he felt very strongly about them. He and Father never agreed. About anything. Especially roses. Plank was a back-to-nature type. He thought that domesticating flowers was cruel and unnatural. You can imagine what my father, a DeRosenquill, thought about that!"

Hermux could imagine Androse DeRosenquill pruning away at Plank with his shears.

"Were you and Plank close?"

"Very close. It hurt me terribly when he left. And it was worse when he didn't come back."

"What happened?"

"I don't know. When he got out of jail, Plank had changed. He just wasn't the same."

"Jail? How did he get in jail?"

"I forgot you don't know your Thorny End history," Primm said. "I'll try to make it short. When my mother's parents died,

64

my mother inherited Jeckel Island. When Plank finished high school, he moved out there. He wanted to go back to nature. He even built a tree house to live in. Father didn't like it, but he thought a little roughing it would straighten Plank out. But before long Plank had a whole tribe of friends out there with him. They lived off the land. They found honey. They gathered berries. I was only allowed to visit there twice. But it made an impression. They all seemed so innocent and so happy."

"So what happened?"

"The town didn't like having a hippie commune offshore. The rock festival was the final straw."

"The Jeckel Island Rock Festival!" Hermux exclaimed. "I wasn't old enough to go, but I've heard all about it. That was your brother who organized it?"

Primm nodded. "Yes. And someone filed a complaint. Apparently it was a very important someone and a very serious complaint. We never found out who did it or why. Thorny End is a small town. You can't do business here for five generations without making enemies. Somebody wanted to teach the DeRosenquills a lesson, and they used Plank to do it. The police broke up the festival and arrested Plank. They held him without bail for thirty days despite everything my father did. Jail broke his spirit. When he finally came home, he hardly spoke to us. Then he took a few things and disappeared. And after that we never heard from him again. That was what my father couldn't forgive. And he blamed Plank for everything else that happened."

"What else did happen?" Hermux asked.

"Plank was my mother's favorite child. She had a nervous breakdown, and she never recovered. And then there was Buddlin. Poor little rich Buddlin. Maybe he never had a chance.

65

As for Plank, as far as my father was concerned, when he left Thorny End, he ceased to exist."

"And what about you?"

"I'm embarrassed to say this, Hermux, but until last week I probably hadn't thought about Plank in years. I haven't had time. For better or worse DeRosenquill and Son is my life. It takes twenty-four hours a day, and it's all I've ever done. It's probably all I ever will do. And now that Reezor Bleesom's perfume is such a hit, I'm going to be busier than ever."

"What happened last week?"

"What do you mean?"

"You said you hadn't thought about Plank until last week. Did something happen?"

"Nothing important."

"Anything might help."

"It was silly. I was at the rose market, visiting one of our customers at Everything's Coming Up Roses, and I bumped into someone — I mean literally bumped into him — who reminded me a little of Plank. It wasn't him."

"What reminded you of Plank?"

"The look in his eyes. Half innocent and half mad. That's how Plank looked the day he came home from jail. He was so sad."

"Did you speak to the man?"

"I started to apologize. But before I could say two words, a young squirrel appeared from nowhere and screamed at me for being clumsy. He was one of those rude-looking boys with spiky fur. Frankly he scared me. I think they were homeless."

"And you haven't seen them again?" Hermux hoped there was more to the story than that.

"No, I haven't."

"It's not much to go on."

"It's not anything to go on," said Primm. "I'll be honest with you. I don't have much hope of your finding Plank. The year after he left, my mother hired a detective. But nothing came of it. I don't know what you'll be able to find after all this time has passed. And I'm not sure I even want you to find Plank, but I'm willing to have you look if only to give my father some peace of mind and some closure."

"Wow," said Hermux. He didn't know where to start. "Do you have any photographs of him? Family pictures?"

"Father destroyed most of them. But I think Mother may have kept a few photos of Plank hidden. I could look. Is there anything else I can do?"

Hermux thought back through everything that Primm and Androse DeRosenquill had told him. "That detective your mother hired. Did he send her a report?"

"I have no idea. What good would it do?"

"It might give me an idea where he looked, at least."

"Hermux, I'm really short on time this week. Reezor Bleesom is throwing a huge party to show off his mansion and his gardens Saturday morning. We're doing all the flowers for it. And today he calls and says that besides the bouquets for the house and the banquet tables, he wants us to build a parade float for him to ride in at the party. All made out of roses. I don't know how I'm supposed to get that done in time. But if I can squeeze a second in, I promise I'll try to look for that report. If I find anything, I'll call you."

"That would be great."

Primm walked him toward the door.

"You seem like a nice mouse, Hermux. I feel bad that we've dragged you into this. I don't want your trip to be a complete waste of your time, so if it's convenient for you, and you're still interested in the project, why don't you go by the clocktower and have a look at it. Then you can tell me how we should proceed. The tower's locked, but they have a key at Boots and Coots. It's a coffee shop near there. Tell them I sent you. Their coffee is good. And so are their donuts."

A donut sounded very good to Hermux.

"I ask one thing, though," said Primm. "Don't mention to anyone that we're looking for Plank. It'll just stir up trouble."

Chapter 15
LOVE AT FIRST BITE

"I'll take two cherry-rosehip-peanut crullers and a cup of coffee."

"Sure you don't want to make it three?" The squirrel at the counter of Boots & Coots Coffee Shop winked at Hermux. "You save twenty-three cents."

"All right," said Hermux. "Twist my arm."

The squirrel scooped the donuts onto a saucer and slid it across the counter.

Hermux took a bite immediately. The first thing he tasted was the sweetness of cherries.

"Are those as good as they look?"

Hermux turned with his mouth full. He was looking into a pair of curious eyes framed by thick, round, black-rimmed glasses. Hermux was surprised to see another mouse. So far, everyone he'd met in Thorny End was a squirrel.

"The reason I ask," the mouse said, "is that I'm throwing a party, and I'm going to be ordering a lot of donuts."

Hermux bit into a tart bit of rosehip. And then a peanut.

"Mmmmmm," he said. He nodded and gave the cherry-rosehip-peanut cruller an ardent thumbs-up. "Delicious!" he managed without spewing crumbs.

"I think I'll order some," the mouse said. He was a bright-looking mouse with fur the color of a vanilla cookie. His clothes were also bright. He wore a red corduroy suit with orange flying saucers all over. Hermux quite liked it. And a red shirt and tie too. "Thanks for the recommendation," he said. "It always pays to ask a local."

"Oh, I'm not from Thorny End," Hermux said. "I'm from Pinchester."

"Me too," the mouse said. "Are you in town for my party? If you aren't, why don't you come? It's on Saturday. I've got a lot to celebrate."

"I'm afraid I can't. I'm here on business, and I'm going home tonight."

"Too bad. It's going to be a good party. I'm showing off my new house. And my new rose garden—I designed it. It's shaped like a rose." He borrowed Hermux's napkin and sketched a quick rose with his pen. "See? And there's a fountain in the middle, right there. My name's Reezor, by the way. What's yours?"

"Hermux Tantamoq. I'm a watchmaker. You're Reezor Bleesom, aren't you? I'm a big fan of Fresh Mown Hay."

Reezor looked pleased. "Thank you. That's a good choice for you," he said. He pocketed the napkin. "I always liked the smell of hay in the morning. I have to go now. I still have to order jam and popcorn and soda. If you change your mind, don't forget—Saturday morning. The roses will be perfect, and there'll be lots to eat."

Reezor ordered ten dozen donuts and gave instructions for delivering them. Then he turned to leave. As he did, he took one of the donuts from Hermux's plate. "It was nice to meet you!" he said. He waved and walked out the door, munching contentedly.

"You know him?" the counter squirrel asked.

"Just met him," said Hermux, taking a new napkin.

"He took one of your donuts."

"I noticed."

Hermux pulled his saucer closer.

Boots & Coots opened with the rose market every morning at four A.M. and didn't close until midnight. The donuts were made fresh twice a day. The coffee was made fresh if you were lucky. The counter showed years of hard use. So did the help and most of the customers.

At the end of the counter sat two old regulars. They watched Reezor Bleesom's departure with evident displeasure.

"More city mice coming to town! Just what we need!" complained one. He made no effort to lower his voice.

"It's not bad enough we got mice," his friend replied. "Now we got an invasion of homeless squirrels too."

"I saw those two last week out at the DeRosenquill place. I was working the front garden."

Hermux didn't intend to eavesdrop, but the mention of DeRosenquill got his attention.

"The old one was marching around big as you please in that raggedy coat of his. I caught him heading right for the front door. Old man DeRosenquill woulda bust a gut if he seen 'em. I run 'em off."

"What'd they want?"

"Don't know. Jobs probably. Like they've ever worked a day in their lives! And the young one's got a temper. He put up quite a fuss."

"I heard they was living under the wharf. That don't sound good."

"Wherever they're living, it's time they start thinking about moving on. I can't tolerate sneakin', stealin', or snoopin'!" As he spoke, he turned his stool to face Hermux.

Hermux hadn't realized it, but as he had been listening to the squirrels' conversation, he had been leaning closer and closer to them. The squirrel pointed at Hermux's nose. "Looks like you'd learn to keep your nose out of other people's business."

Hermux jumped.

"I didn't mean to snoop," Hermux tried to explain. "But I couldn't help hearing you talk about the DeRosenquills. You see, I may be working for them. I'm a watchmaker. And they're planning to repair the clock in the Old Clocktower."

"I heard about it," the old squirrel said, and looked at Hermux with new interest. "Say, maybe you could fix my pocket watch." He fished a clumsy-looking timepiece from his overalls. "It runs kinda slow. It's been years since we had a watchmaker in Thorny End."

But before Hermux answered, the other squirrel interrupted.

"There he goes!" he said. He pointed out the front window.

Across the street a scruffy-looking squirrel hurried toward the market. He presented an odd figure for Thorny End, and his fur stood out in spikes.

"Who is it?" asked Hermux.

"It's the boy. The one I saw at the DeRosenquills."

"Surely that's not a boy," said Hermux. "He looks too old."

"No. That's him all right. The one with the temper."

Chapter 16
EVERYTHING'S COMING UP ROSES

The squirrel had a two-block head start, and Hermux would have to push hard if he wanted to catch up. He threaded his way along the crowded street, dodging delivery trucks and scooting around crates, all the while keeping the squirrel's spiky head in sight. Before long, he was huffing and puffing. Linka might be right. Maybe it was time to cut down on donuts.

Then somewhere just past the rose farmers' supply store the squirrel disappeared. Hermux continued on, scanning the sidewalk ahead of him and checking each side street he passed. But there was no sign of him. Hermux turned around and began to retrace his steps.

And there he was. He must have gone into one of the shops. The squirrel waited at the curb as a line of tractors pulling empty rose wagons rolled past on their way out of town. Hermux worked his way toward him. He was almost near enough to speak when the squirrel darted between tractors and raced across the street. Hermux started to follow, but the procession of tractors picked up speed. There were no more openings.

Maybe it was just as well, Hermux thought. He wasn't sure exactly why he had followed the squirrel in the first place. All he had was a hunch to go on. The squirrel's partner had reminded Primm of Plank. It wasn't much of a clue, but Hermux had agreed to take the case and it was the only clue he had.

Hermux scanned the shop signs along the street. One of them had a familiar name.

Everything's Coming Up Roses

WHOLESALE ONLY

Hermux walked inside and found an empty store. A low counter crossed the room. Behind it an open doorway led back to what looked like a warehouse and a loading dock. The only spot of color in the room was a wall calendar with a picture of June's rose of the month—a lavish pink hybrid tea rose. The air was pungent with roses, and Hermux's nose prickled with pleasure—a welcome sign that his nose was beginning to recover.

A squirrel's head poked in from the warehouse.

"Wholesale only!" he said. He pointed toward the door. "It says so outside. No exceptions. And I *don't* want to hear about your wedding budget. It's not my problem."

"How did you know I was getting married?"

"Everybody tries to save a buck!"

"But wait—I'm not here to buy flowers," Hermux informed him. "I had a question about a squirrel who I think was here. He's kind of punk looking with spiked-up fur."

"Don't remember anybody by that description," said the shopkeeper, who was obviously not the cooperative type.

"Are you sure? Dressed all in black?"

"Doesn't ring any bells." The squirrel stifled a yawn. "Is that all?"

Hermux was ready to give up when he spotted a bulky canvas bundle on the floor behind the counter. He pointed it out to the clerk.

"He must have been here. He was carrying that bundle."

"Oh, *that* boy," the squirrel said. "He's not here."

"Is he coming back?"

The squirrel tore open a package of roasted acorns and tossed one in his mouth. "Who's asking?"

Hermux gave him his card.

"A watchmaker, huh? He run out on a bill?"

"No. No. It's personal. I just wanted a word with him. Will he be back today?"

"He comes and goes." The squirrel ate another acorn.

"You don't happen to know where he lives, do you?" Hermux asked.

"He's not the talkative type."

"Do you know his name?"

"Couldn't say," the squirrel said. He cocked his head and looked at Hermux.

He seemed to be waiting for something. Hermux got out his wallet. He laid a six-dollar bill on the counter and looked away. When he looked back, it was gone.

The squirrel smiled.

"Feeling more talkative?" Hermux asked.

"Roses," the squirrel said. "The boy sells roses. Wild ones. He brings them in every day about now." He hoisted the bundle up on the counter and opened it for Hermux to see.

A cloud of fragrance enveloped Hermux and the clerk. Hermux recognized it immediately. His nose throbbed a sharp warning, and he jerked his hand away from the counter. The squirrel's wild roses were the same as Mrs. Thankton's.

75

"I recognize these roses!" said Hermux.

"Not likely," said the squirrel. "They're very rare. We've got one customer who buys them all."

"I know! Mrs. Thankton in Pinchester!" The unexpected connection sent a ripple of excitement down Hermux's spine. "Where do you think the boy gets them?"

"Hold it right there, mister!" The squirrel had stopped smiling. "Did Mrs. Thankton send you down here?"

"What do you mean?"

"You know what I mean. To cut me out of the loop and buy directly from the boy."

"No!"

"Then why are you asking questions about the roses?"

"I wasn't. I was asking about the boy. It has to do with a missing person."

"Oh," the squirrel said. "Is there a reward?"

Hermux opened his wallet and counted his cash. "How about seventeen dollars?"

The squirrel pocketed the money. "All right," he said. "Here's what I know. They showed up a month or so ago, the boy and an older guy, with these wild roses. I feel sorry for the boy, so I help 'em out. I think they're getting the roses out on the island."

"Jeckel Island?"

"Right. From the old Jeckel gardens."

"You mean you think they're stealing them?"

"Nobody's cared about those roses for years, so I wouldn't exactly call it stealing. But I warned them not to get caught. They don't like trespassers on the island."

Hermux thought about the young squirrel. It couldn't be easy to be homeless. But it would be even worse if he wound up in jail for trespassing and stealing roses. Hermux wasn't sure why he suddenly felt responsible for a boy squirrel he had never met, but somehow he did. He remembered the gardener's story of chasing the two squirrels away. "Did you tell them to go out to the DeRosenquills and ask permission to pick the roses?"

"The DeRosenquills? Why would I do that?"

"It's their island, isn't it?"

"Oh, no. They haven't owned it for years. Old man DeRosenquill sold the island as soon as his wife died. The Institute for Positive Thinking owns it now. They've never been friendly. And the new management is even worse."

Chapter 17
ON DUE REFLECTION

Hermux spotted a pay phone across the street and was eager to call Primm. As he walked toward it, a white van squealed up to the curb and cut him off. A businessmouse in a nut brown suit jumped from the van and ran into the phone booth.

"Sorry!" he said. "It's an emergency!" He slammed the door in Hermux's face.

Hermux stood there for a moment, uncertain what to do. The businessmouse slid the door open again.

"Do you mind, buddy? This is personal! Beat it!"

Hermux moved down the sidewalk away from the phone booth. Then he found a shop window where he could see both the phone booth and the van reflected in the glass. Inside the booth he spied the mouse thumbing through the phone book. Inside the van, a large, tough-looking squirrel was dozing in the passenger seat. Hermux deciphered the lettering on the van's side, and laughed when he read:

THE INSTITUTE FOR POSITIVE THINKING
BUILDING BRAVE NEW WORLDS WITH THE
POWER OF THOUGHT!

The shopkeeper had been right. The institute's new management wasn't the least bit friendly.

Chapter 18
CUTTING CORONERS

It took Killium two tries to find the number he wanted. *County Coroner . . . Th2-4399.*

He dropped three coins in the phone and dialed while he got himself into character. Dialing the number brought back pleasant memories from his childhood. He had entertained himself for hours on end with nothing but a phone and a phone book. The line rang and rang. When someone finally answered, Killium was sorely tempted to ask him if his refrigerator was running. But he stopped himself, assumed a very professional tone, and said, "I'd like to speak to the coroner, please. This is Riggin O'Ronius calling long distance from the Keester County Sheriff's Office."

A voice responded, "I'm not sure I ever heard of Keester County."

"We're used to that," said Killium jovially. "We're pretty small potatoes down here. You big city fellas don't pay us much attention."

"Thorny End is not exactly a big city."

"Depends on what you're used to, I guess." Killium was having a grand time. "Anyways, I'm calling to do you folks a favor. I understand you've got an unidentified body on your hands."

"As a matter of fact, we do. I'm planning to perform the autopsy this evening."

"You're lucky I called, then. I can save you some time. An autopsy won't be necessary. I sent a van up there this afternoon. They'll swing by and have the body out of there in no time."

"But I haven't determined the cause of death yet."

"Oh, there's need for that. The poor guy drowned. He fell off his boat three days ago. Purely accidental. I've got four witnesses, including the wife. Poor woman. The current must have swept him north. Anyway, the family wants to hold the funeral tomorrow. That's why we sent the van up. I'll take care of all the paperwork on our end."

"Well, it's a little irregular," said the coroner.

"Nope. It's as regular as can be. I guess we do things a little different down here. But since he died in Keester County, he falls under my jurisdiction."

"I'd have to let the mayor decide that. He's got his mind set on an autopsy."

That was not what Killium wanted to hear.

"Give me your number," said the coroner. "And I'll have the mayor call you back. You two can work it out."

Killium thought fast. "I'm going to be in and out today. Why don't I call him direct? Have you got that number?"

Dutifully Killium wrote down the mayor's number. Then he hung up the receiver and stared blankly at the street.

It was time to go to Plan B.

Unfortunately, Plan B didn't exist.

Chapter 19
PROFESSIONAL COURTESY

Hermux wandered through the market. The street was lined with shops for every imaginable rose product from rose-flavored candy to rose-scented room freshener. There was a rose book-store and even a shop that sold artificial roses. But Hermux found one shop near the end of the street that had nothing to do with roses. It appeared to be an art gallery. In the window was a dis-play of sculpture. Hermux's eye was drawn to one in particular. It was a very realistic ladybug that bore a striking resemblance to Terfle. She was splendidly carved and painted, standing on a pear twig. Hermux thought it would make a splendid present for Terfle. Since she was becoming an artist herself, it might be time for her to start her own art collection.

Hermux examined the piece more closely. The craftsmanship was superb down to the smallest detail of the bark on the twig. Hermux was used to small work himself, and he was impressed. He studied the ladybug's face. It was so lifelike that Hermux wouldn't have been surprised if it had smiled. Then he realized his mistake. It wasn't a sculpture at all. It was a real ladybug. It had been stuffed and mounted.

"Yuck!" Hermux said. He stepped away from the window.

But he was too late. The shopkeeper had seen him and was already hurrying toward the door.

"Come in! Come in!" he said, taking Hermux by the arm and pulling him into the store. "I'm sorry I didn't see you sooner. I was on the phone. Are you shopping for yourself or someone special?"

He was a squirrel a few years past middle age, but due to the hazards of his profession, he looked considerably older. He suffered from chronic fur loss as well as several itching and splotching disorders of the skin. He pushed his glasses up on his head and gave his ear a quick scratch before offering his paw to Hermux.

"Pleased to meet you," he said. "Thirxen Ghoulter — professional taxidermist — at your service."

Hermux introduced himself as well. "I'm visiting from Pinchester," he added.

Hermux's handshake wasn't quite as firm as usual, and when he was done, he wiped his hand unobtrusively on his pants.

"I can already see you're partial to ladybugs. But before you make a decision, I want you see my spiders. I'm famous for my spiders, if I do say so myself!"

Hermux found himself eye to eye with a woolly spider the size of a suitcase. He tried to squirm away, but Thirxen locked a scaly paw on his arm and pulled him even closer.

"You like tarantulas? This one's a beaut! I'm particularly proud of the fangs."

From that distance the tarantula's fangs looked as big as grappling hooks.

"I can give you a good price," Thirxen said. "A local dentist shot it last year on a hunting trip to the Great Desert. But his wife won't let it in the house."

"Well," said Hermux. "I'm not sure—"

"That's okay! There's plenty more." He moved Hermux right along. Next to the tarantula, a sleek black creature with spindly legs drew itself up in a menacing pose. Beneath it on the shelf Hermux saw a small mirror.

"Check it out!" Thirxen told him. "I call her Big Mama! She's my pride and joy."

Hermux leaned close for a better look. In the mirror he could see the red hourglass that marked her abdomen.

"Black widow!" sang Thirxen. His fingers scrabbled playfully across Hermux's bent back. Hermux jerked upright and started for the door, but Thirxen blocked the way.

"Okay! Okay! No spiders. We'll stick to the cuddly bugs. What about a beetle?"

"I don't think so," said Hermux.

"Butterfly?"

"No."

"A bee?"

"Definitely not!" Just the thought of bees made Hermux jumpy.

"I've got a great selection of bees. Honeybees, carpenter bees, bumblebees. Nothing is cuddlier than a bumblebee. Makes a great present for a child."

Hermux didn't answer. He was thinking about the bees.

"Then I guess it's the ladybug."

"No. I've already got a ladybug. A live one. She's my pet."

"You should consider getting her stuffed. They're a lot less trouble stuffed. No food. No cage to clean. No vet bills."

"No, thank you," said Hermux firmly. "I like her the way she is. But I might take a look at your bees after all."

Thirxen led him to a specimen cabinet and pulled out one of

its wide drawers. The drawer was divided into square compart-ments. In each compartment lay a bee. As Hermux examined the first bee, each element of its anatomy blossomed into exquisite detail. He moved to the next bee and the next, his interest and excitement growing.

"They're beautiful!" he said.

"Ah!" said Thirxen. "A bee man! I should have known. Looking for anything in particular?"

"Do you have any local bees?" asked Hermux.

"Local, regional, national, and global," said Thirxen. "I'm a bee man myself."

"I'm looking for a really big local bee. Maybe something from Jeckel Island?"

"You're a collector, then? Why didn't you say so? I can give you a ten percent discount. But I don't have anything from Jeckel Island right now. Can't get 'em anymore."

"Why not?" asked Hermux.

"New management over there. Even crankier than before. They don't like visitors."

"I've been hearing that. What is the Institute for Positive Thinking, anyway? What do they do on that island? And why are they so unfriendly?"

Thirxen pulled his glasses down and situated them on his nose. He looked at Hermux through the thick, smudged lenses. "Tell me something, Mr. Tantamoq. What brings you to Thorny End?"

One of the first challenges Hermux had had to face as a private detective was the occasional necessity of stretching the truth, especially if he was working undercover. In this case, he wasn't undercover. At least not yet. And despite Thirxen's peculiar profession and moth-eaten appearance, he seemed like a decent fellow. Hermux thought it might be helpful to have an ally in Thorny End. He decided to be frank.

"Strictly between you and me?" he asked.

"One professional to another," Thirxen assured him. "By the way, what is your profession exactly?"

"Normally I'm a watchmaker," said Hermux. "But recently I've been working as a private detective. This is my fourth case. A missing person."

"A watchmaking detective? Interesting. So where does the bee fit in?"

"I'm not really sure. It's just a hunch."

"I'm working on an interesting case myself right now. Might be a bee angle there too."

"What you do mean?" asked Hermux.

"I'm the county coroner," he said. He flashed a badge.

"You're kidding!" said Hermux.

"Not really. Somebody's got to do it. And I'm the only one around here who isn't squeamish."

The phone rang then, and Thirxen went to answer it. "It might be the mayor," he told Hermux.

But it wasn't. It was Reezor Bleesom. Reezor's new house had a pool for water lilies, and Reezor wanted dragonflies to go with it. So far none had shown up. So he had ordered twenty dragonflies custom stuffed for his party. The party was less than two days away now, and he was getting worried because they still weren't ready.

Thirxen reassured Reezor that his order would be ready in time.

"I'm afraid I can't talk any more right now," he told Hermux.

"I still have three more dragonflies to stuff, plus the wings to mount, and they take a lot of time. But tell you what. Are you going to be in town tonight?"

"I am, as a matter of fact. I'll be here until nine o'clock."

"Good," he said. "Come back about seven thirty. I may have something for you on the bee angle. Something very interesting."

Chapter 20
WHAT'S UP, DOCK?

During the glory days of the Institute for Positive Thinking, the institute's van was a familiar sight on the narrow streets of Thorny End. Arriving guests were met by van at the airport and whisked to Jeckel Island via the institute's own private ferry. The guests no longer came, but the institute still maintained the ferry. It hadn't much choice. Jeckel Island lay a mile offshore in the center of Thorny End Bay, and the ferry provided its only access. Like the institute, the ferry had seen better days. But the engine was still reasonably reliable. At least it was if Skuhl was around to tend to its peculiarities. Skuhl had worked for the institute from the day it opened its doors. Besides tinkering with the ferry's engine, Skuhl did as little as possible. He was a great believer in conserving energy. That afternoon he was conserving energy by sleeping in the sun on a large crate on the ferry's deck. He was awakened by the rumble of the van on the uneven timbers of the dock. He sat up in time to see the van coming onto the ferry and heading directly at him.

He hoped he was dreaming. But to play it safe, Skuhl put up his paws and yelled, "Stop!"

At the wheel of the van, Killium noticed nothing. He was driving on autopilot. He wasn't expecting a crate to be sitting in his parking place on the ferry. His thoughts were occupied with more important things, like figuring out a plan.

Just then Hanger woke up from his nap in the passenger seat.

"Brakes!" he screeched. "Now!"

Through his daze Killium heard him, and he slammed on the brakes. The van skidded to a stop just inches from Skuhl's quivering kneecaps.

Hanger reached for the van's keys and turned off the engine.

"That's cutting it close, boss!"

"That's my spot! What's a crate doing there, anyway?" Killium leaned out the window and repeated his question, louder this time, for Skuhl's benefit. "I didn't tell you to put a crate there! It would have served you right if I'd hit you."

"Where was I supposed to put it? It's addressed to you. 'Personal and private,' it says." Skuhl was beginning to recover his wits.

"Well, I didn't order it!" Killium retorted. "Get it out of the way."

"Not so easy, boss," said Skuhl. "It's heavy. Took three guys to get it off the truck."

Killium turned to Hanger. "Help him."

Hanger got out.

"*Three* guys," said Skuhl. "And none of them was runts." He eyed Killium's new suit. "Or your fancy executive types."

"All right. All right. I'll help," said Killium. He climbed down from the van, took off his new jacket, and folded it carefully.

"What is it, anyway?" He walked around it to get a better look at the crate. Stenciled on its side was a notice:

WARNING: CONSULT YOUR PHYSICIAN BEFORE USING THE
SURVIVAL OF THE FITTEST HOME GYMNASIUM®

"Is that for us, boss?" Hanger asked. He struck a bodybuilder's pose. Then he turned to Skuhl. "We got promoted to security! We're gonna get uniforms too!"

"Great!" said Killium sarcastically. It was a gym. And it was for him. Tucka and her workout program! He was so irritated that he was tempted to dump the crate right in the bay. It looked like a coffin, so why not bury it at sea? He snorted at the thought. It would serve her right! Then he stopped. He took another look at the crate. And Plan B began to take shape.

Ten minutes later the ferry departed for Jeckel Island. The crate was loaded into the van. The van was parked in its usual spot.

Hanger and Skuhl waved at Killium as he pulled away from the dock.

"You're sure he can pilot that thing?" asked Hanger.

"I guess we'll find out. How much money did he give you for dinner?"

"Thirty bucks."

"Wow! That is one weird mouse. One minute he nearly runs me over and doesn't even apologize. And the next minute he's giving us the rest of the day off and treating us to dinner. What's going on?"

"Top secret. New assignment from headquarters."

"Where is headquarters, anyway?"

"How would I know? Let's go shop for uniforms. I want all camo with plenty of straps."

"We get guns too?" asked Skuhl.

"You bet!"

"Do we get to shoot 'em?"

"We got orders to shoot on sight." Hanger jumped forward, turned, dropped into a marksman's crouch, and drew a two-handed bead on Skuhl. "Bang!" he said. "You're dead!"

Chapter 21
DARK AT THE TOP OF THE STAIRS

Hermux had read about the Clocktower when he was at watch-making school. At the time it was built, it was a marvel of clock-making.

Now Hermux gazed up at the tower. Even in disrepair it was an impressive structure. Built of red brick, it loomed over Thorny End. It was square, and at the top of each side was a clock face. Each face was made of stained glass designed in the shape of a rose. They were originally red, pink, white, and yellow roses. But these colors were now hidden beneath the layers of grime that had accumulated over the years.

Hermux tried to imagine what it used to look like in the morning sun. Or the glow of evening. Once a great lantern had lit the tower from inside at night, silhouetting the clock hands against the shimmering colors of the glass.

But now the hands pointed haphazardly at some forgotten hour.

"It's a shame," he thought. "It must have been so beautiful. It would be an honor to be the watchmaker who was chosen to restore it."

Hermux decided to take advantage of the remaining light and get a good look at the mechanisms of the clock.

Hermux reached the door of the tower just as he realized that he had forgotten to ask for the key when he visited Boots & Coots. He had left in too big of a hurry. Then he realized that the key wouldn't be necessary. The tower door stood slightly ajar. Hermux pushed, and it opened with a rusty rasp. He poked his head inside.

"Hello?" he called. "Is anybody here?"

From far overhead came an answering creak.

"Hello?" Hermux repeated.

There was still no answer.

Hermux stepped inside. The tower was even gloomier than the Villa DeRosenquill. He felt along the wall for a light switch but found nothing. Overhead there was another creak. Hermux raised his head and looked up. A very faint light showed above. Like the light at the end of a long tunnel. But this tunnel rose straight up. Hugging the tower walls, a narrow staircase spiraled upward and vanished into darkness. Hermux tried the first step. It seemed solid enough. And the second as well. Mercifully a banister ran along the wall, although apparently it was designed for squirrels and was mounted a bit too high to be comfortable for Hermux. Still, it was a comfort to have something solid to hang on to as he climbed up into the blackness. He clung to it with a firm grip until it ended inexplicably somewhere past the halfway point.

Hermux stopped. The light was slightly stronger now, and his eyes had adjusted to the darkness. He could make out more steps at least. That was a help. And his hearing, always keen, had intensified. He was certain he heard someone above. The telltale scrape of a shoe on the floor. The rustle of paper. The sound of chewing. And then his nose twitched. He smelled peanut butter. Unmistakably. Someone in the tower was eating a peanut butter sandwich. It smelled delicious.

"Hello?" he said. "Hermux Tantamoq here! I'm here to take a look at the clock."

No answer.

"Not very friendly," thought Hermux. "I wonder if it's another watchmaker?" Sliding his hand along the wall, he continued up. The light grew stronger. Hermux turned the last corner and saw that the next flight of stairs led to a trapdoor in the ceiling. The door was propped open.

"Thank goodness!" he said. He climbed up quickly. His first impression, on stepping into the room, was that he had stepped into an aquarium. The air shimmered with color that filtered down from above. It was the light from the rose windows of the clock faces. Even dulled and caked with dirt, they glowed.

"Oh, my!" said Hermux. Then he saw the clockworks, covered in dust and shrouded with cobwebs. "Oh, my!" he said again. This time he did not sound so enthused. "Still, I supposed it could be worse." At least he didn't see any obvious rust.

The smell of peanut butter was stronger now. It was mixed with a hint of smoke. Hermux looked around but saw no one. Then he saw a sleeping bag. And another. An orange crate set like a table beneath one of the windows. On it was the stub of a candle and an open jar of peanut butter with a knife still in it. Next to the peanut butter lay a battered copy of *The Runaway Squirrel*. That was a good sign. It was one of Hermux's favorite books.

"I know someone's here," he said. "You may as well come out!"

Hermux heard a twang, and then something struck his leg. It struck hard, and it stung like fire.

"Ow!" said Hermux.

Then a figure emerged from the shadows and shoved Hermux to the ground. Hermux raised his head just in time to see the squirrel with spiky fur scramble through the trapdoor and vanish below.

Moments later the tower door slammed shut with a boom that echoed up through the dark, empty space, and then slowly faded away.

Chapter 22
PARTY LINE

Killium's laboratory was located in the barn of the old Jeckel farm. The barn had been converted to classrooms by the institute. Tucka had converted the classrooms to labs. Everything was state of the art, including the library, which was extensive and included books about botany and biology and chemistry and biotechnology.

Tucka would be coming to Thorny End the day after tomorrow. Killium had promised her a spectacular surprise for Reezor's party. But he had no idea what that would be. He took down one of his own most treasured reference books and opened it to the table of contents. He had always found it inspiring.

THE THINKING MAN'S GUIDE TO
PRACTICAL JOKES

PROFESSIONAL EDITION
(with new chapters on Cruel, Vicious & Dangerous Pranks)

Unfortunately, this time it all seemed pretty ho-hum.

The Vomit Punch sounded promising. But what if Reezor didn't use a punch bowl?

The Laxative Soup could be fun. But it would have to be extremely fast acting, or it wouldn't ruin the party.

And Tucka had been very definite about ruining Reezor's party.

It was too bad he couldn't use the killer bees. He glanced out his window toward the greenhouse. That would be a party Reezor wouldn't forget! But the bees were off limits now. And he didn't even want to think about them just then.

He was getting nowhere when the phone rang. It was Tucka.

"So?" she said. "Have you been thinking of me? I've been thinking of you."

"I have," he said. He had thought of her several times. Particularly when he put his hand on his wallet, which was where he had put her check for twenty-five thousand dollars.

"And have you been thinking about Reezor's big surprise?" There was a hint of a warm growl in Tucka's voice.

"Nonstop," he said. He closed his eyes and stabbed a finger at the open book on his desk. "What would you think about a—" He opened his eyes and read from the page. "A fart bomb?"

There was dead silence on the line.

"What did you say?" Tucka asked. The warmth and the growl were gone. Replaced by an Arctic cold front.

"Just joking!" Killium reassured her.

"I'm not in the mood."

"Sorry," he apologized. "Oh, by the way, talk about big surprises—the gym came!"

"Do you like it?"

"Like it? I'm totally pumped," he told her. "Can't wait to get started!"

"Don't get too muscular," she teased. "I'll have to order all new suits for you."

"Maybe a set of new wheels too," Killium suggested. "Something sporty?"

"You don't ask for a lot, do you?" Tucka laughed. "Don't worry. I know how to show my appreciation. But first let's see how Reezor's party goes. If you make me really happy on Saturday—who knows?"

"And what would it take to make you really, *really* happy?" He was a fast learner.

"I'd have to think about that," said Tucka. She thought for a full five seconds. "I guess what would really make me happy would be to arrive at Reezor's big party with all the other guests and the reporters and the photographers and to see the expression on his face when he realizes that every single last rose in his fabulous rose garden is as dead as a doornail."

"I see."

"I thought you would. And I'm going to need a Lip-Fix before the party. It will be the perfect opportunity to announce it to the public. After a tragedy like that, people always appreciate some good news."

Chapter 23
UNIFORM BEHAVIOR

In the heyday of Thorny End, what the locals referred to as the Rosy Years, tourists came from all over the world to enjoy the colorful spectacle of the rose harvest and savor the valley's exquisite rose-scented sea air. There were many hotels, but the Inn at Thorny End was undoubtedly the finest. When the Rosy Years came to a close, it was the only one to survive. The inn was superbly located. It sat at the south end of town, across the Paddlepick River, surrounded by gardens and overlooking the point where the river flowed into the bay. A small bridge crossed the river, connecting the inn to the town.

Hermux stood in the middle of the bridge and looked upriver. The sun had begun to set in the west, changing the sky from blue to gold. It was so beautiful that Hermux wished that Linka were there to see it with him. So soothing that he forgot for the moment just how much his leg hurt.

He didn't forget for long. That squirrel had hit him with something hard, and Hermux had a huge bump to show for it. It was the size of a walnut and located just below his knee. He felt it every time he took a step. Luckily it wasn't much farther to the inn.

The dining room at the inn was busy. The waitress was a chubby, cheerful squirrel with a very sweet face. She had an extravagantly fluffy tail, the long hairs of which, despite the fur-net she wore, hovered distractingly just above her sparkling black eyes.

"I've only got two tables left, you can take your pick," she told Hermux. "You're lucky you came tonight, though. Tomorrow night we're booked solid. VIPs from Pinchester. There's a big party on Saturday. And they're all coming down for it."

Hermux chose the booth by the window so he could look out at the bay.

The waitress asked, "Can I get you something to drink?"

"Yes, you can," Hermux said. "I'd like a strawberry lemonade if you have it."

"Fresh made!"

"Thank you!"

She handed him a menu and started for the kitchen.

Before Hermux opened his menu, he took a moment to appreciate the view. Out in the bay lay an island.

"That must be Jeckel Island," thought Hermux.

Although the sky was beginning to darken, Hermux could see what looked like a dock and a boat on the island's nearest shore. Beyond that the beach gave way to a forest. As he watched, a bank of fog rolled in and the island seemed to shift and change shape. The dock faded, and then the beach, and then the forest. Then a gust of wind tore at the curtain of fog, and a last ray of sun lit the scene. Hermux stared at the island in disbelief. And a pair of sightless eyes seemed to stare right back. What had been an island was now only patches of shadow and mist. But the patches had assumed the unmistakable form of a skull. A leering skull with a twinkle in one eye.

Then the twinkle moved. The fog shifted again. The island reappeared, and Hermux smiled in relief to see that the twinkle was in fact the headlights of a car driving down toward the dock.

A hand touched Hermux's shoulder, and he jumped despite himself.

"Here's your lemonade, hon! Did you decide on dinner?"

"No," said Hermux. "Sorry! I was watching the island."

"Looks like fog."

"Yes, it does," said Hermux.

"Wouldn't want to be out there tonight!"

"Me either. But how come?"

The waitress brushed her tail away from her eyes and gave Hermux a sharp look. "Don't get me started on that!" she said. "You want to hear the specials?"

He did. He ordered the watercress and turnip soup and the cheese potato with a small salad on the side.

"Good choice," commented the waitress.

"And I've got a few questions about the inn when you've got a chance."

"Sure," she said. "*If* I get a chance."

Hermux went over the list of Linka's wedding questions after the waitress left to put in his order.

She was soon back with the soup. And it was delicious. While he ate it, Hermux watched outside. The bay was dark now, so he turned his eyes toward shore and the twinkling lights of downtown Thorny End and, looming above it, the dark outlines of the clocktower. He wondered if the young squirrel had gone back up there. He could be there now, reading *The Runaway Squirrel* by the light of a single candle. The dismal old tower seemed like a poor place to call home, but it might be safer than the street.

He was pondering that when the cheese potato appeared. After one bite of cheesy goodness all thoughts of the squirrel and his plight were forgotten. Hermux even forgot about the ache in his knee. He smiled happily. At least he had one answer for Linka. The food at the inn was very good. He pushed his empty plate away, unfolded his list of questions, and waited for the waitress to return.

"Dessert?" she asked as she whisked his plate away.

Hermux remembered the day's donuts. "I'm afraid not. But I would like to ask —"

She was already gone.

"I'll be back in a sec," she called over her shoulder.

She returned, leading two squirrels in uniforms. She seated them in the booth next to Hermux, dropped Hermux's check in front of him, and rushed back to the kitchen.

One of the squirrels had a particularly loud voice. Hermux couldn't help overhearing him.

"That's a tail on that one, huh? And she definitely liked my uniform! Women are suckers for uniforms."

"Let's face it, Hanger, you're irresistible with or without the uniform." The other voice wasn't quite so loud, but it was clearly audible.

"I'm telling you, the uniform makes a difference," the first squirrel said. "I can already feel it."

"Yeah, I can feel it too. A big difference. It's uncomfortable. Tell me again what we're doing. It doesn't sound like much of a promotion."

"We're beefing up security. From now on no one sets foot on the island without the boss's orders."

As far as Hermux knew, there was only one island near Thorny End.

The second squirrel sounded skeptical. "No one's been on the island in months except for those two homeless squirrels. And what harm are they going to do?"

"It's not what they do that matters. What matters is what *we're* going to do."

"And that is?"

"We're gonna shoot 'em! We got guns now, and we're supposed to use them."

"Sounds like a lot of extra work to me. And nobody's mentioned extra pay."

"Shooting's not work. It's fun."

"How would you know?"

"Well, at least I intend to find out."

Hermux did not like the sound of that. Despite the fact that the spiky young squirrel had inflicted considerable injury on him, Hermux didn't think he deserved to be shot. He was just a boy, after all. Hermux would have stayed to hear more, but he remembered his appointment with Thirxen Ghoulter the taxidermist. He stood up, taking his time to put on his jacket and get a good look at the two squirrels in uniform. Except for their uniforms, there wasn't much to distinguish them in Hermux's eye from ordinary, run-of-the-mill squirrels. The loud one was the younger of the two. The other was older and pudgier and appeared altogether less excitable. Before they noticed him, Hermux turned and walked to the cash register. The waitress met him there.

"Everything okay?" she asked.

"Delicious!" said Hermux.

"Didn't you have some questions?" she asked.

"I did," said Hermux. He lowered his voice. "Those two gentlemen there. The ones in uniform. Are they with the army?"

"Army!" she hooted. "Those two bozos work at the institute on the island. They're Dr. Wollar's so-called assistants."

"What do they do?"

"Do?" She made a face. "As far as we know, they don't do anything. They're both lazy bums."

"Why do they have guns?"

"Guns! Heavens! Now you're making me nervous. I wouldn't trust those two with peashooters!"

"And who's Dr. Wollar?"

"He's the new director. Sneaky and cheap. Your typical mouse! I call him Dr. Joker." She brushed her tail back from her eyes. "I'm sorry! That was rude of me. You seem like a very nice mouse. He's not!"

"I understand," said Hermux. Squirrels and mice were known to have their differences. "What does the institute do, anyway?"

"Executive Potential Enhancement. That's what they used to call it. They even held a workshop for us at the hotel. 'Better service through positive thinking.' It was more fun than working, that's for sure." She smoothed the fur-net on her tail and tried for an optimistic smile. "Those were the days. Lots of nice people coming and going. Good tippers too! But that all changed with the new owners. Who knows what they do out there now!"

"Where does Dr. Wollar fit in?"

"Not here, that's for sure. Last week the good Dr. Joker left me a fifty-dollar tip."

"That's generous, isn't it?"

"Not in play money it's not. But I'll get even."

"How?" asked Hermux.

"I have my ways," she said mysteriously. She flicked her tail

103

toward Hanger and Skuhl. "Our friends in uniform are about to get a taste."

"What are you going to do?"

"I.S.I.T.S."

"What does that stand for?" asked Hermux.

She whispered, "I spit in their soup."

The chef's bell rang. "Order up!" he sang. "Two soups!"

"Duty calls!" the waitress told Hermux. "Have a nice evening, hon. And you come back and see us, you hear?"

Chapter 24
A BONE TO PICK

Hermux left the inn and walked back toward town.

Hermux opened the door of the taxidermy shop and recognized the figure of Thirxen Ghoulter sitting at his desk inside, reading a book. "Hello there!" he said. "I hope I'm not too late!"

"Late?" asked Thirxen. "I wasn't expecting you back at all." He did not seem very happy to see Hermux.

"Why not? You said to be here at seven thirty. You said you might have some information for me. About bees?"

"Now it's bees, huh? What about my black widow?" He closed his book and put it down. He glared at Hermux. "Well?"

Hermux glanced at the book.

AUTOPSIES FOR IDIOTS
THE ILLUSTRATED STEP-BY-STEP GUIDE

"I'm not sure I follow," said Hermux.

"Big Mama's gone!"

"You think I stole your black widow?" Hermux couldn't believe it.

"You were the last one here!" Thirxen said accusingly.

"What would I do with a stuffed black widow?"

"You've got a girlfriend, don't you?" Thirxen asked unexpectedly.

"I have a *fiancée*," Hermux corrected him. "But what does she have to do with it?"

"A spider like that would make a heck of a present! Give it back!"

"I assure you I did not take your spider." Hermux was indignant. "First of all, I don't steal. Second, I don't like spiders. Especially black widows. And neither does Linka. And third, no offense, but neither of us likes stuffed animals. We like them alive!"

"Hmmmph!" answered Thirxen. "They're a lot more trouble alive!"

"Trouble or not, that's the way we like them!"

"Well, all right," Thirxen grumbled. "Maybe you didn't take it. But she's still missing."

"I'm very sorry," said Hermux. "Have you been here the whole time?"

"I stepped out for a bite to eat. But I locked up."

"Is there a back door?"

Thirxen nodded. "But it's always locked."

Hermux wasn't sure he had time to take on a new case just then. He had to meet Linka at the airport at nine o'clock. He decided to change the subject. "You said you were working on a case yourself. Something with a bee angle? Did anything turn up?"

106

"Didn't get to it yet. But since you're here, you may as well help. Ever done an autopsy?"

"A what?" Hermux squawked.

"Autopsy. Dead squirrel washed up on the beach this week. The mayor wants to know what killed him. You're a detective, aren't you?"

"But you're the coroner!"

"Sounds like we'd make a good team. I'll read you the directions. You do the cutting."

Hermux thought about it. "How about I read the directions? And you do the—whatever."

"Squeamish, huh?" Thirxen smirked.

"No more than normal," Hermux defended himself. "But I want to know the bee connection first."

"You'll see," Thirxen told him. "Follow me. And bring the book." He led the way to the back of the shop. Hermux passed by the case with the tarantula. Sure enough the space next to it was empty. The black widow was definitely gone. An odd idea for a gift. But then Thirxen was definitely an odd fellow.

A heavy curtain covered the door to the back room. Hermux pushed past it and found himself in pitch darkness.

"Where are you?" he asked.

A disembodied voice answered. "I think a lot about murder, you know."

"You do?" said Hermux.

"It's a fascinating subject. Don't you think?"

"I suppose so. You want to get the light?" Hermux did not particularly want to talk about murder in the dark.

"For example, this evening I was thinking what a perfect place for a murder a morgue would make. Don't you agree?"

"You want me to get the light?" Hermux asked.

"Who would suspect a coroner? And there are so many ways of getting rid of a body. Knives and saws. I think I've even got a grinder here somewhere."

"Is it a pull string or a switch?" Hermux asked.

"And I've got beetles that will eat anything. Did you tell anyone you were coming here tonight?"

"Plenty of people!" Hermux lied.

"That's a pity!" said Thirxen. The lights went on. He was standing not a foot away from Hermux with a scythe-shaped stainless steel saw.

"What are you doing?" yelped Hermux.

"Just testing. Did you take my spider or not?"

"I did not!" Hermux insisted. He was struck suddenly by the strange, stark beauty of Thirxen's saw. Its teeth glittered in the fluorescent light. Each one was at least an inch long and looked as sharp as a dagger.

Thirxen stared deeply into Hermux's eyes. Then he put down the saw.

"Okay!" he said cheerfully. "I believe you. But I had to be sure. I got your attention, didn't I?"

"You did," Hermux admitted.

"No hard feelings, right? Now help me get the squirrel up on the slab. We've got four refrigerator drawers. I think they put him in the first one."

Unwillingly Hermux followed him to a bank of white metal drawers. Thirxen pulled the first one open. It was empty.

"That's funny. I guess it's the next one."

He opened the second drawer. But it was empty too. Then the third. No luck. Slowly he slid the fourth drawer open.

There was nothing there.

"It's gone!" he gasped. "The body is gone! It was here this morning!"

"I don't doubt you," said Hermux. "Let's go back to that first drawer. I think I saw something."

Thirxen pulled it open.

"What's that?" Hermux asked. He pointed to the foot of the empty drawer. Crumpled on the shiny steel surface lay a very large bee.

Chapter 25
ANATOMY LESSON

"Somebody must have broken in and stolen the body," Hermux said. "Look. The back door has been pried open. See where the wood is splintered? Whoever did it used a crowbar. They could have sneaked in when you went to dinner. What's outside?"

"The loading dock and the alley."

"They must have driven right up," said Hermux. "And then driven off with the body."

"Like curb service," said Thirxen. "But why would someone steal a body?"

"And take a black widow too," Hermux reminded him.

"I already told you it would make a great gift."

"Right. A gift." Hermux didn't sound entirely convinced. "So what kind of person steals a body and gives black widows for gifts?"

"A sick one?"

"Possibly," said Hermux. But he was thinking. "You were planning to do the autopsy tonight, right? Did anyone else know that?"

"Well," Thirxen began. "The mayor for one. He's anxious to avoid a panic. Then there's Reezor Bleesom. I mentioned it to him on the phone this afternoon. He didn't seem too interested, though. And there's that sheriff who called from Keester County. He didn't want an autopsy at all. He claimed to know the victim *and* the cause of death. He was supposed to call the mayor and clear it. But I didn't hear back from him."

"Where's Keester County?" Hermux asked.

"Somewhere south of here. On the coast."

"I don't think so," said Hermux. "I've never heard of it." Both Hermux and Terfle were great appreciators of maps. They had spent many a winter evening poring over the pages of Hermux's great atlas. Hermux had an excellent memory for detail. He visualized all the counties on the map of the coast south of Thorny End. There was no trace of a county called Keester.

"Maybe he was wrong about that," said Thirxen, shaking his head. "He was sure wrong about the cause of death. I don't think that squirrel drowned."

"What do you think happened?"

"Bee stings. That squirrel was covered with them. He was swollen up like a balloon."

"And you think the bee in the drawer was one of the bees that killed him?"

"Makes sense to me," said Thirxen.

They moved the bee's body to the front room and placed it on the brightly lit worktable. Thirxen and Hermux took turns examining it.

Even to Hermux's untrained eye it was obvious that this bee was related to the one that had stung him on the nose at Mrs. Thankton's shop. It was the same size and color. He recounted the story and held up his nose for examination.

"I wondered about that," Thirxen said. "I thought you might be a drinking mouse. In my experience detectives like a tipple now and then. Must be the pressure."

"I do not tipple," said Hermux. "Especially on the job."

The bee yielded several unusual details to Thirxen's expert eye. It reminded him of a bee in his collection. He found the specimen and brought it over for comparison.

"Look," he told Hermux. "The bee from my collection is quite a bit smaller than our bee. But notice the shape of the wing. They both have this little notch there." He pointed it out with the tip of a scalpel. "And the hair along the hind legs. On both of them the hair is tipped with gold."

That reminded Hermux of the markings he had noticed at Mrs. Thankton's.

"What about their stomachs? Mine had markings."

Thirxen gently turned both bees over. With his magnifying glass he could see that the abdomen of the specimen bee showed some vague gold marks in the black fur. The large bee was quite a different story entirely. The marks were sharp and bold.

"Looks like letters," said Thirxen.

"Indeed," said Hermux. The letters were not IM as he had thought before. He could clearly read a T and an M plus the symbol ®. It looked very familiar. Then he recognized it. "It's a trademark."

"On a bee?" Thirxen was shocked.

"I'm afraid so. Where did you get the specimen?"

"Why, I collected it myself. Years ago. Out on Jeckel Island."

"What do you think is going on out there?" asked Hermux.

"I don't know. But look at this." He pointed the scalpel at the big bee's rear end. "See where the stinger broke off? That was no ordinary stinger. It was enormous, even for the bee's size. These bees have mutated. It wouldn't take that many to kill you. That must be what happened to that squirrel."

Chapter 26
CAN YOU DIG IT?

At the wheel of the ferry Killium felt alive as he never had before. He was a mouse of purpose now. A mouse of means. Twenty-five thousand dollars' worth of means and more to come. He stood proudly at the wheel — the captain of his own ship, rushing boldly forward to meet the unexpected head-on.

And so he did. The ferry slammed into the dock with a hard thump. Killium pitched forward against the wheel. The ferry gave a violent shiver. The dock groaned. There were sounds of scraping and creaking. But, miraculously and no thanks to Killium's seamanship, the dock held. The ferry heaved to a stop.

"Home from the sea!" he announced with satisfaction. "Not bad for my first solo night crossing!"

Killium swaggered on deck, tied off the ropes, and lowered the loading ramp, whistling all the while. Then he got in the van and drove it off, following the narrow road that led from the dock up to the old Jeckel farmhouse, now the main building of the Institute for Positive Thinking.

He parked the van in the garage and moments later emerged with a shovel in hand. He was thinking very positively just then. "Show me a problem, and I'll show you a solution," he boasted to the empty night as he made his way toward the front of the house.

Killium had hatched his plan that afternoon on the dock in Thorny End. The plan was simple, bold, and direct. In fact, it was perfect. It required only a van, a crate, a crowbar, and plenty of nerve. All of which he had. "Oh!" he said. "And a shovel. Let's not forget the shovel."

He planted said shovel at the base of a rosebush in the garden below his bedroom window. He set his foot on it and dug in. The dirt was a lot harder than he expected. He was soon panting from the exertion. After ten minutes he had dug up four rosebushes. He was drenched with sweat, and his new handmade suit was covered with dirt. After fifteen minutes he had managed to dig a small rectangular hole in the ground and tear a large triangular hole in his suit.

Killium paused to reconsider all his options. The other obvious option had been burial at sea. But after his first experience in trying to dispose of a body at sea, he had decided against it. The tides had proven unpredictable. Besides, it was too late for that now. The barbells of the Survival of the Fittest Home Gymnasium®, which would have provided excellent weight, had been dumped in the bay to make room in the crate. Perhaps it had been a mistake. A small flaw in his otherwise perfect plan. But that wasn't a positive way to think about it. And Killium intended to keep a positive attitude. There was really only one option. And that was to dig a hole big enough to hold the crate and conduct a private and informal funeral service before the sun came up tomorrow.

By three in the morning, he had finished the hole. He climbed out wearily and trudged off in the direction of the van. He was at the entrance of the garage when he realized that his perfect plan might have a second small flaw. He could have dug the hole closer to the van. He wasn't sure he had the strength left to haul the crate all the way around the house. Squirrels were heavy. And this one in particular was dead weight.

But a creative mind like Killium's is never idle. "A good hot shower is what I need now," he told himself. "Then I'll be good as new."

And it turned out that he was right. To a point.

He took a long shower, letting the hot water pulse against his back and his shoulders. He felt kinks in muscles he didn't even know he had. But soon those kinks began to loosen in the warmth that enveloped him. He felt physically rejuvenated. And mentally too. He was thinking clearly again and positively. That might explain why, when he emerged from the bathroom, wrapped in a towel and a cloud of steam, and saw his bed with its pillow so white and soft and the blanket turned back so invitingly, it only took him a moment to make another executive decision. He would set his alarm for one hour and take a short, revitalizing nap.

Then he would get up and finish the job with plenty of time and energy to spare.

Chapter 27
NIGHT FLIGHT

With only one commercial flight a day, Thorny End's airport was a small informal affair, not much more than a Quonset hut and a wind sock. Hermux was looking forward to the flight home and a good night's sleep.

Prompt as always, Linka was there waiting for him.

"You poor thing!" she said when she saw him approach. "You're limping! What happened?" She put her arms around him comfortingly.

It felt very good to Hermux.

"It's a long story," he told her. "Several long stories, in fact. I'm not sure I remember it all."

"You look exhausted. Let's get you in the plane and take you home."

It was music to his ears.

Once in the plane, Hermux settled back in his seat and watched Linka with a mixture of awe and respect as she methodically prepared for takeoff. Linka was an expert pilot, and Hermux, who not did particularly care for heights or airplanes, no longer worried about flying, as long as he was flying with her.

The airport was beyond the reach of the fog, and they were

soon airborne. Below them the streetlights and porch lights of Thorny End thinned out and gave way to darkness. Lit by moonlight, the Paddlepick River glittered in the dark like a vein of silver leading west. Above them the sky was black and filled with stars.

For a while neither of them spoke. It was enough simply to be together again, suspended, as they often found themselves, midway between heaven and earth. It was hard for Hermux just then to believe that a world of such beauty could also be a world of sadness and fear, disappointment and loss. But those were the themes that had filled his day.

"I'm just so happy to be with you," he said to Linka. "We're so lucky. And I'm very grateful."

Linka reached for his paw and squeezed it.

"I'm grateful too," she said. "Do you want to tell me what happened?"

He was so tired, he didn't know where to begin. "I'd rather hear about you."

"Well," said Linka, "I had a pretty good day. I saw four inns. The Whispering Pines Lodge was beautiful, but I don't think we can afford it. The other three were okay. They have their strengths and weaknesses. I took good notes. We can go over them tomorrow. What about the Inn at Thorny End?"

"The soup was good," Hermux said as his stomach took a dip.

"What about the rooms? And the kitchen? And the dates? What do they have available?"

"I'm not sure," said Hermux after an uncomfortable pause. "There's a nice waitress, though."

"Did you even ask?" Linka sounded a little impatient.

"I forgot," he admitted miserably.

"You forgot?"

"I know," he said miserably.

"Really!" Linka sighed. "I don't know what to say!"

"I don't either."

"Hermux, sometimes I wonder if you really want to get married at all."

Chapter 28
DIRTY WORK

The morning was dreamy. The sunlight was bright but not glaring. The breeze was cool but not cold. It was a perfect morning for snoozing. As Killium burrowed beneath the covers, he dreamt of money. Piles of crisp, green one-hundred-dollar bills. He dug to the center of the pile and hollowed out a cozy nest. Then he curled up and went to sleep. Killium was happy there. He did not wish to be disturbed.

But disturbed he was.

First there were voices. Then there was much clomping about. And then there was complaining. The sound of someone complaining can be very irritating.

It was so irritating to Killium that he finally woke up. He had a headache and a terrible crick in his neck. He covered his head with his pillow. "Shut up!" he grumbled. "I'm trying to sleep!" But the voice went right on complaining. Killium ground his teeth.

The voices were coming from outside. He stumbled groggily to the window, pushed back the curtains, and threw it open. He leaned out and yelled, "Shut up, for pity's sake!"

The morning light came as a shock to Killium's eyes. But

not as shocking as the sight that greeted him below. A rectangular hole had been dug in the center of the rose garden. Next to the hole stood Hanger and Skuhl in their uniforms. Hanger had a shovel in hand and was vigorously refilling the hole with dirt. Skuhl was leaning on his shovel, complaining about the extra work.

"We nearly caught 'em, boss!" Hanger shouted up. "Somebody must have sneaked over last night to steal roses! If they come back, we'll be ready for them!" He patted the pistol in his holster.

Killium looked at his clock. It said nearly eleven. The alarm was set for 4:00 A.M. He had slept right through it.

"Stop!" Killium bellowed down to the men. "Stop it right now!"

Skuhl dropped his shovel instantly. "What'd I tell you?" he said.

Hanger was confused. "I thought you'd want it cleaned up, boss."

Killium scrambled for an explanation. It came to him in a flash.

"You're destroying evidence, you nincompoop!"

"Right!" Hanger said humbly. He was awestruck by Killium's superior knowledge of crime scene procedure. "Why didn't I think of that?"

"Because you don't think?" Skuhl muttered beneath his breath.

"Don't touch anything, either of you!" Killium ordered. "I'll be right down." He ran to the bathroom and frantically splashed cold water on his face. "Stay calm!" he told himself. "It will all work out!" He toweled off and threw on his suit. He was pulling on his socks when there was a terrific crash downstairs. It shook the entire house.

121

"Now what?" he wondered. He hopped into his shoes and headed toward the stairs. When he reached the living room, he found Hanger and Skuhl. Between them in the center of the room sat the wooden crate.

"Sorry, boss!" Hanger apologized. "It's a lot heavier than I thought. You want us to set it up?" He reached to open the lid.

Killium's eyes bugged. He crossed the living room in two giant steps, slapped Hanger's hand away, and threw himself across the crate. "Keep your hands off it!" he said.

Skuhl shrugged. "I told you we should leave in the van."

Hanger looked hurt. "We're just trying to help, boss. I thought you'd want it set up right away so we could all work out together."

"Somebody please help me!" Killium implored.

Before anyone could, the phone rang. Nobody moved to answer it.

"You want to get that, boss?" Hanger asked cautiously.

"No, you get it," said Killium. He refused to leave the crate.

Hanger walked to the hall and answered the phone. He was back in a moment. "It's for you, boss. It's a lady."

"Stay away from the crate," Killium warned. "It was a present. I get very sentimental about presents."

"I get it," said Hanger. "From a lady. Right?" He nudged Skuhl and winked.

"Right," said Killium. He picked up the receiver.

"Dr. Wollar speaking. May I help you?"

"It's me."

"Who?"

"Tucka, silly! Guess where I am."

"I have no idea," said Killium.

"I'm at the airport!" she said.

122

"Where are you going?" he asked.

"I'm not going anywhere. I've already arrived. I'm in Thorny End! I wanted to surprise you."

"You did," said Killium tonelessly. While he watched it, the crate in the living room seemed to grow in size. He was evidently having a nightmare. He tried to slap himself awake but only succeeded in hurting his face.

"Send the van out for me right away!" Tucka told him. "I can't wait to see what you've got for the party."

Chapter 29
UP TO SPEED

"And when we opened the drawer, the body was gone," Hermux said. He snapped his fingers. "Vanished into thin air."

No one said a word. The only sound in the shop, besides the ticking of at least seventy-three clocks, was the faint scratch of Terfle's pencil on her sketch pad.

Then everyone spoke at once.

"Where do you think it went?" asked Nip.

"Do you think the security guards shot him?" asked Beulith.

"No wonder you forgot to ask about the inn!" said Linka. "I'm sorry I snapped at you!"

Hermux responded to Linka first. He lowered his eyes modestly and tried to look as lovable as possible. Then he told Nip, "Somebody stole the body. They jimmied open the back door." Then he told Beulith, "He wasn't shot. He was stung to death by mutant bees. The same kind that stung me."

Nip regarded Hermux's nose uneasily. Hermux recounted what he and Ghoulter had found when they examined the bees. Then he added, "I think the bees are on the island. That's where the boy is getting the roses."

"But why?" asked Linka. "Why did the bees mutate? Why would someone steal the body?"

"I think it has something to do with the island and the institute," said Hermux. He reached across the counter and snagged the last plain chocolate cake donut from the box. He bit into it and took a sip of coffee. Lanayda Prink still made a tasty donut, but it didn't compare to a cherry-rosehip-peanut cruller. "And there's one more thing."

"What?" asked Linka.

"We found this mark on the bee's stomach." He removed a piece of paper from his wallet, unfolded it, and laid it out on the counter. On it was a drawing.

"What is it?" asked Nip.

"It's Tucka Mertslin's trademark," said Beulith.

"I am never buying another product from that woman!" Linka vowed.

"Her lipsticks are awfully nice," said Beulith.

"So's her nail polish," said Linka. "But there are limits! She's a menace to society."

"What's the connection?" asked Nip.

"I'm not sure," Hermux said. "But my nose tells me that she's mixed up in this somehow."

"If she is, that young squirrel could be in danger," said Nip. "Tucka's ruthless."

"Even if she's not, he's in danger," said Hermux. "If the bees don't get him, the guards will. One of them is definitely trigger-happy."

The sound of Terfle's pencil stopped. Hermux peered into the Port-a-Pet where she sat at her drawing table.

"How are you doing in there?" he asked her. "Are we boring you?"

Terfle shook her head violently. She held up her sketchbook.

"Can we take a look?" asked Hermux.

She looked away bashfully, then carried her sketchbook to the door.

Terfle was continuing her efforts at action drawing. As Hermux flipped through the pages with the tip of his little finger, he saw himself, Linka, Nip, and Beulith seated on stools pulled up to the counter. They were chatting, drinking coffee, and eating donuts. Then he turned another page and found himself face-to-face with an angry-looking teenage squirrel whose fur stood out in wild spikes. He was quite a dashing character. Perhaps a little more dashing than Hermux remembered.

"This is very good," he told Terfle. "You really captured his likeness. Even his angry expression." Hermux passed the sketchbook and the loupe on to Linka. And one by one they each examined Terfle's drawings.

"Glissin told me that you had talent," Beulith exclaimed to Terfle. "But I had no idea! These are wonderful! Could I get one blown up? I'd love the one of Nip and me together."

Terfle was very pleased.

"That's an excellent idea!" said Hermux. "I could get one of the boy blown up. It might help us find him."

Beulith took another look at the squirrel's portrait. "He's cute!" she said.

Terfle nodded in agreement.

"If you like the angry-young-squirrel type!" Nip groused.

"I do!" said Beulith. "He'd look good onstage. You think he can act?" Beulith and her father ran the Varmint Variety Theater, and they were always on the lookout for talent.

Linka broke in. "First, I think we'd better get him out of there before he gets hurt."

"So you're going back?" asked Nip.

"I think we have to," said Linka. "Hermux has taken the case. And besides, I need to visit the inn. We still have a few questions to ask them." She winked at Hermux and smiled.

Chapter 30
CAMOUFLAGE

Hanger picked Tucka up from the airport and drove her to the island. She wasn't quite what Killium had described.

Tucka was in disguise. She didn't want to be seen in Thorny End before Reezor's party. That way no one could point the finger of blame at her if something went wrong. And she intended something to go very, very wrong. Her chauffeur would drive down tomorrow morning and pick her up near the ferry. She would change in the car and arrive at Reezor's with all the other guests. She would look fresh and innocent and terribly surprised. In the meantime it would be best not to draw any attention to herself. So for the flight down she has dressed simply and unobtrusively.

As he drove, Hanger kept an eye on Tucka in the rearview mirror. Occasionally their eyes met. He was pretty sure she liked his uniform. He definitely liked hers.

Tucka wore a blond wig teased up high in front that fell in loose ringlets over her shoulders and halfway down her back. With that she had on a red velvet cutaway jacket—the type that circus ringmasters prefer. It had giant gold buttons and oversized black cuffs and long tails in back. Under that she wore black patent-leather pants and high-heeled, knee-high, lace-up boots. She had brought three large suitcases with her. She wouldn't be there long, but she intended to enjoy her stay on Jeckel Island.

"So what brings you to Jeckel Island?" he asked.

"Didn't Dr. Wollar tell you?" she asked.

"No, ma'am, he didn't. He just told me to pick you up, pronto."

"Oh, the sly rascal!" she said. "He's such a tease. I'm his cousin, his kissin' cousin. You can call me Keenkie." She cracked her gum and rewarded him with a little squirm.

"Yes, ma'am!" said Hanger. He licked his lips. "Whatever you say!"

"Shouldn't you be watching the road?" she asked. "I think that's the ferry ahead."

It was indeed. Hanger braked just in time and the van squealed to a stop on deck.

Chapter 31
NO PICNIC

Killium had already had several surprises too many that day. So when the blond ringmaster stepped into the living room, puckered her substantial lips, and said, "Aren't you going to give your cousin Keenkie a little kiss?" Killium was speechless.

Tucka crossed to him and gave him a demure peck on the cheek.

"Surprised to see me?" she whispered. "But what's this? A picnic? How rustic!"

Killium had thrown a tablecloth over the wooden crate. He'd picked a handful of roses and put them in a pickle jar and set out paper plates and cheese and jelly sandwiches. Tucka grabbed a sandwich and was about to eat it when she noticed Killium's suit. It was covered with dirt and torn now in several places. She put her sandwich down.

"Tell me that's not your new suit!" she demanded.

"We had an emergency."

"That's right, Miss Keenkie," Hanger butted in. "Intruders! Stealing the roses. But don't you worry!" He slapped his holster. "We got you covered now!"

"Intruders?" Tucka asked. "That doesn't sound good."

"It's all taken care of," Killium assured her. "Shall we eat?"

Skuhl arrived then, staggering under the weight of Tucka's luggage, which he promptly dropped on the floor.

"Where do you want these?" he asked.

"Oh, I want the Honeysuckle Haven!" Tucka said. "It's my favorite cabin. I always stayed there."

Skuhl looked to Killium for instructions.

"You heard the lady. And Hanger, you go with him."

"Sure, boss!" said Hanger. "I'll check it out for security. Don't worry, ma'am, you're safe with me here."

"I don't doubt it," said Tucka. She gave him a pout. When they were gone, she asked, "How much do they know?"

"Next to nothing," said Killium.

"And the intruders?"

"Just kids. A prank. Nothing to worry about."

"He's kind of cute in that uniform." Tucka watched for Killium's response. There wasn't any. "You're not jealous, are you?"

"Of that clown?" Killium was regaining his equilibrium. "I don't think so!"

"He *does* have a gun," said Tucka. Then she remembered the Survival of the Fittest Home Gymnasium® "Where did you set up the gym? I can't wait to see it."

"I've got something I want to show you first," he stalled. "I got you a little present."

"For me?" Tucka grabbed a hank of blond hair and twirled it seductively. "What is it?"

"Wait here and close your eyes."

Tucka closed her eyes and waited. She loved presents.

Killium returned shortly.

"Put out your hands," he said.

She did.

"All right! You can open your eyes."

There in her hands was the biggest black widow she had ever seen in her life. She screamed.

"I love it!" Then she thought about it. "It's dead, isn't it?"

"Totally!" said Killium. "It's stuffed."

A large mirror hung in the hall. Tucka ran to it. She poufed up her blond wig and then placed the black widow on her head like a tiara. She studied the effect. And then she turned and smiled at Killium. It was a deadly smile.

"Come here, Killer!" she said.

He approached her cautiously. When he was within reach, she grabbed him with both hands and kissed him right on the mouth. It was not a very cousinly kiss.

Chapter 32
FAMILY ALBUM

Terfle had no intention of staying home and missing an entire adventure. Hermux tried to reason with her. His first day on the DeRosenquill case had been very strenuous. And dangerous too. It was likely to get worse. But Terfle was adamant. Hermux argued that he couldn't very well carry the Port-a-Pet around with him all day long. It was too bulky and heavy. And that was when Terfle played her trump card. Just the week before she had seen an ad in the *Daily Sentinel* for Puppit's Pet Shop. They were running a special introductory offer on the Sport-a-Pet. It was the latest thing in travel accessories for adventure-loving pet owners and their pets. Ultralight and smaller than a backpack. Perfect for hiking, camping, and sailing. The sale ended that day.

Reluctantly Hermux gave in. After all, Terfle had been very cooperative in letting him make a blowup of her drawing of the squirrel. And so that afternoon, as Hermux and Linka walked up the steps of the Villa DeRosenquill, Terfle rode along proudly in a small padded cage that Hermux wore like a backpack.

"Can you see okay?" Hermux asked.

Terfle rang her bell. The view from the Sport-a-Pet was

stunning. Despite a touch of motion sickness, the sight of the DeRosenquill gardens had her salivating.

The butler wasn't any nicer than he had been the day before, but he led them straight to Primm's office without delay. Primm arrived a few moments later, out of breath.

"I'm glad you got my message," she said. "I have a few things for you."

Hermux introduced Linka and Terfle, setting the Sport-a-Pet on the corner of Primm's desk.

Primm leaned forward. "I'm glad to meet you," she told Terfle. "So you're an associate detective, are you? Well, detective or not, ladybugs are always welcome at Villa DeRosenquill." She turned to Linka. "And you're the adventuress, aren't you? I've read about you. I've always wanted to travel myself, but I've never been able to get away from here."

"It's so beautiful here," said Linka. "I can see why you might not want to leave."

"Oh, I want to leave!" said Primm. "But Father's not well, and there's always a crisis. Tomorrow is Reezor's party. My best picker is out sick. We're not done with the bouquets for Reezor's house, and we haven't even started on his float. I don't know why I ever agreed to do it. I must have been crazy." She rubbed her forehead with a dirt-caked paw.

"I didn't sleep well," she continued. "This thing with Plank is bothering me. I had a horrible dream. Father blamed me for everything. He screamed at me, 'If it weren't for you and that book, he would never have run away!' "

"What book was he talking about?" Hermux asked.

The Runaway Squirrel."

Hermux, Linka, and Terfle exchanged curious looks.

"I gave it to Plank for his ninth birthday," said Primm. "After

134

he read it, he always wanted to live in a tree house. It's funny, isn't it? How life turns out?"

Hermux tried to tell her about the homeless squirrel and the danger that he and his partner were in. But Primm didn't have time to listen.

"I'm sorry," she said. "I've got to get back to work. Can it wait until tomorrow? Perhaps you can come back then? Or we could speak by phone?" As she rose to leave, she removed an envelope from her desk and handed it to Hermux. "I did manage to find one picture of Plank. A family photo. It's not much. Can you find your way out?"

"No problem," said Hermux.

And then she was gone.

"She looks tired," said Linka sympathetically.

"I think she works very hard," said Hermux.

Then Primm was back. But only for a second.

"I also found an old letter from the detective agency," she said in a rush. "It's in the envelope. I forgot to tell you. But I doubt that it says much."

Chapter 33
ARRESTED DEVELOPMENT

Hermux opened the envelope. Inside was a letter and a black-and-white snapshot of a group of squirrels—two elderly squirrels in old-fashioned clothes and three children. They stood together on the porch of a white frame house. The two elderly squirrels looked both dignified and proud. The oldest of the three children, a girl with her fur in braids and her teeth in braces, smiled hopefully at the photographer. One of her hands rested firmly on the shoulder of the boy next to her—the youngest—who was making a horrible, sour, angry face. The third child was also a boy, close to the girl in age. He appeared somewhat disheveled and perplexed, as though he were uncertain about the whole business of posing for a photo. He reminded Hermux of pictures he had seen in the *Weekly Squeak* of tribal squirrels captured on film for the first time by explorers in faraway places like Teulabonari.

"There's writing on the back," said Linka.

Hermux turned the photo over.

Summer, Jeckel Island
Grandmother and Grandfather Jeckel, Primm (age 14),
Buddlin (age 5), and Plank (age 12)

He handed it to Linka.

"The happy family," she said. "Plank looks like he's from another planet."

"Buddlin looks a little odd too."

"Why do little boys make faces like that?" Linka wondered.

"Maybe she's pinching him."

"Maybe he deserved it," she teased.

Terfle rang her bell then. She wanted a closer look at the photo. Linka held it up for her while Hermux opened a faded envelope addressed to Mrs. Fenilope DeRosenquill. The letter inside was typed on onionskin paper. He unfolded it and read.

PRYHARD PRIVATE INVESTIGATORS

PROGRESSIVE BUILDING
Pinchester

Dear Mrs. DeRosenquill:

I have completed my inquiry into the arrest and imprisonment of your son Plank DeRosenquill as per your request. As you know, both the police file and court records were sealed at the time of your son's arrest. Using careful undercover work and quite a few expense account dinners at the Inn at Thorny End, I was able to gain the confidence of a courthouse clerk. While she was not able to obtain copies of the documents in question, she did provide me with access to them and I was able to examine them carefully and reconstruct the events in question.

August 12: A complaint against Plank DeRosenquill for vagrancy, criminal trespassing, and general mischief was

---

filed with the Thorny End police department by Androse DeRosenquill, his father, acting in the interest of the Jeckel family estate.

August 13: Thorny End police officers raided the commune on Jeckel Island, arrested Plank DeRosenquill, and evicted the remaining residents.

August 14: Androse DeRosenquill testified against his son in a secret, closed session of the court and prevailed upon the judge to sentence his son to a month of solitary confinement in the county jail to, in his words, "teach him a lesson he won't forget and pound some sense into that thick skull of his."

August 15: Plank DeRosenquill was placed in solitary confinement, on reduced rations, and denied all visitation rights.

September 15: Plank DeRosenquill was released from jail.

I hope this information will be of use to you. Please let me know if I may be of further assistance.

Attached you will find my invoice for $500 plus a detailed accounting of reimbursable expenses.

Yours very truly,

Penton Pryhard

Penton Pryhard

"Five hundred dollars!" exclaimed Hermux. "And that was fifteen years ago. I had no idea detectives charged that much!"

"For what?" Linka asked.

Hermux gave her the letter. Terfle had finished studying the photo and had started working on a new drawing.

"Primm was wrong," he said. "Her mother didn't hire the detective to find Plank. She hired him to find out who put Plank in jail. And it was Androse, his *own father*, her *own husband!* No wonder she had a nervous breakdown."

"So Androse blamed Plank for the family falling apart," said Linka. "But it was his fault all along. And he knew it! Why, I'd like to give him a piece of my mind!"

"I think it's time we do just that," said Hermux. "Let's go see him. I'll bet he's in the greenhouse."

As Hermux slipped on the Sport-a-Pet and fastened the straps, Terfle rang her bell again. She wanted to show her drawing.

"We don't have time right now," he told her. "We're going to talk to Primm's father."

Chapter 34
FATHER KNOWS BEST

Androse DeRosenquill sat in his wheelchair at the workbench of his greenhouse, still pruning roses. He looked up at the sound of their approach.

"Old man's work," he grouched. If he was surprised to see Hermux, he didn't show it. He was, however, happily surprised to see Linka. Androse DeRosenquill had a soft spot for attractive young women. He sat up, straightened his shoulders, and fluffed his tail. He clipped a rosebud from the bush he was pruning. Then, fixing Linka with a virile, bucktoothed smile, he rolled toward her, rosebud in hand.

"Welcome to Villa DeRosenquill, Miss—"

"Perflinger," she said. "Linka Perflinger."

"Soon to be *Mrs.*," Hermux added protectively. He pointed out Linka's garnet ring. "She and I are engaged."

"Too bad," said Androse. He handed her the rosebud anyway and then rolled back to the table and returned to his work.

"And this is Terfle," Hermux said, indicating the Sport-a-Pet. "She's a ladybug. And my associate."

Androse ignored Terfle and spoke instead to Hermux.

"So you're back," he said. "I assume this means you have news. I hope it's good news."

"There have been developments," said Hermux uncomfortably. He looked to Linka for help.

"Regarding Plank's disappearance," Linka said. "Or rather, his arrest and imprisonment."

Androse stopped snipping.

"Plank's arrest is old history, Mr. Tantamoq," he said coldly. "Perhaps I did not make myself clear yesterday. His arrest is not the subject of your investigation. You were hired to find him and bring him home. And that is all. Is that understood?"

Hermux nodded. "However," he said, "in discussing the case with Primm, she seemed to think that Plank's arrest played a major part in his decision to leave. Which is why—"

"Primm was in no position to judge."

Linka spoke up then. "It seems that your wife shared her views. She even hired—"

"How dare you talk about my wife!" Androse thundered. "She's dead! You have no right to come here and meddle in my family affairs!"

"We are not meddling," Hermux said firmly. "First of all, you invited me here. As a matter of fact, you insisted. Then you told me that Primm would handle all the details. Well, she handled them. And we followed up on them. And we found out what happened when Plank disappeared. And we think it's important."

Terfle's bell tinkled in a show of support.

Androse raised his snips and glared defiantly. "I can't see what possible relevance any of that could have."

"How about this for relevance?" asked Hermux. "It was *you* who had Plank arrested. It was *you* who had him held in jail to teach him a lesson—to break his spirit so he would come home like an obedient child and take his job at DeRosenquill and Son."

"And it backfired," said Linka. "Your son left."

"Plank was a weakling!" Androse's face was rigid with anger.

"And then your wife found out it was you," Linka said. "And it broke her heart."

"She never suspected!" said Androse. The hand that held the snips trembled slightly.

"You're right," said Linka. "She didn't need to suspect. She *knew*. She had proof."

"So what else are you hiding about Plank?" Hermux demanded.

"Get out!" said Androse. "All of you! Get out! You're fired!"

Chapter 35
FOOD FOR THOUGHT

"Maybe we could have handled that better," said Linka.

Hermux stirred his coffee and stared at his plate. He had hardly touched his cherry-rosehip-peanut cruller. "I doubt we could have done it much worse."

"You might have punched him in the nose," Linka suggested. She nudged Hermux.

"I hadn't thought of that." Hermux smiled. "What came over us, anyway?"

"We weren't thinking. We got mad. Even Terfle was mad. You should have seen the look on her face when he threatened you with his snippers! And Androse didn't exactly help."

"So it wasn't entirely our fault?" Hermux's spirits rose. He took a nibble of the cruller. It was every bit as good as he remembered. Tart and crunchy and sweet.

"Not entirely our fault," said Linka. "But mostly."

"Okay," Hermux said. "The next time we have sensitive information about a case, we'll think about it for a while before we do anything."

"Good plan!" Linka tried her cruller. "Mmmmmn. You're right. This *is* good. Do you think they'd give us the recipe?"

"I don't know." Hermux's thoughts were still on the case. "So what do we do now? We're fired. What do we do about the boy? We can't just desert him. And what about the bees? And what do I do with this letter from the detective? I can't very well give it to Primm. And I don't want to give it to Androse."

"Let's take our own advice."

"Which is?"

"The letter contains very sensitive information. Let's think it over carefully before we do anything."

"Good idea. And what about the family picture? I should probably send that back to Primm."

While Hermux and Linka were talking, Terfle had been busy drawing. As she worked, she followed their conversation. Now she put down her pencil and reached for the cord to her bell. She had been ignored long enough. She gave it a sharp pull.

"What?" asked Hermux. "Do you need water?"

Terfle held up her sketchbook.

"Did you get some nice sketches of the greenhouse?" Hermux asked. "I thought you'd like it!"

Terfle scowled. For some reason Hermux was being unusually dense. She had noticed that it happened sometimes when donuts were concerned. She shook her head.

"All right! All right!" said Hermux. "I'll take a look." He took the sketchbook from her and got out his magnifying loupe. Terfle had left it open to a close-up she had drawn of the photo of Plank and his family. She had zeroed in on the young, angry Buddlin DeRosenquill. But she had made a significant change. She had drawn his fur in sharp spikes. Suddenly he looked very familiar to Hermux.

Terfle tapped her foot impatiently. Hermux turned the

page. He found a drawing of Androse DeRosenquill in his wheelchair, brandishing his pruning shears. His face was contorted into an angry mask. Terfle had drawn his fur in spikes as well.

"Take a look at these!" he told Linka. He handed her the loupe and the sketchbook. He fumbled in his jacket pocket for the blowup he had made of Terfle's drawing of the squirrel boy. He studied it a moment and then laid it out for Linka to see.

"Way to go, Terfle!" he told her. "I didn't see it. I guess I haven't been paying enough attention!"

Terfle couldn't keep from nodding in agreement.

"Clever!" said Linka. "There's definitely a resemblance! But what does it mean? And what should we do?"

Hermux thought it over. "I guess before we do anything at all, we'd better think about it. I don't want to go off halfcocked again."

"Good idea," said Linka. "See? We're already making progress."

To facilitate his thinking, Hermux ordered another cruller. Plus a refill on coffee. Linka stuck with coffee. Terfle broke open her lunch box and ate a handful of candied aphids.

They thought hard for five minutes. Then they compared notes.

"What worries me most is the boy," said Hermux. "I think I should try to find him and warn him to stay away from the island."

Terfle was in complete agreement. She hadn't stop worrying about the boy since she had drawn his portrait. She had, if the truth be known, developed a terrible crush on him.

"What I'm wondering about is the institute," said Linka. "If Tucka is really connected, we're going to need some proof. Maybe while you look for the boy, I'll pay a visit to the courthouse and see if I can dig anything up on the current owner of the island."

Chapter 36
PAPER TRAIL

The County Records Office was located in the basement of the courthouse. Except for a matronly squirrel seated at a desk behind the counter, it was deserted. She was listening intently to the radio while she filed her nails.

"I hope you can help me," said Linka. "It's my first day on the job. I'm supposed to research the title on a piece of property in Thorny End."

"Don't let me stop you," said the clerk. She went back to filing her nails.

"I really need this job," Linka confided. "I'm not sure where to look."

"Back there," said the clerk. She pointed her nail file toward what looked like an endless bank of filing cabinets. "It's all alphabetical. And put everything back exactly the way you found it."

Linka thanked her and started to leave. Then she stopped. "Excuse me," she said. "But alphabetical by what?"

"By owner," the clerk said. She was very proud of her filing system.

"But I don't know who the owner is," Linka said. "That's what I'm supposed to find out."

"Then you're out of luck, honey."

"Do you mind if I look?"

"It's a public office. Help yourself."

Linka walked to the first cabinet and opened a drawer. It was filled with folders. She removed one and examined it. Inside was the title and bill of sale for a house in the name of a Mr. Arid Antwhistle. She read it and then carefully returned it to its place, under the watchful eye of the clerk. Linka waved her fingers and then moved on. She would start with the name Jeckel.

It was a smart choice. The Jeckels had amassed a very large file. At the back of it was a copy of a bill of sale for Jeckel Island dated fourteen years earlier and signed by none other than Androse DeRosenquill. The purchaser was the Institute for Positive Thinking.

Linka moved on to the I's. She discovered that the Institute for Positive Thinking had sold the island a year ago to a company called IPT Partners of Pinchester.

Then only a month later IPT Partners sold it again to BV Ventures, also of Pinchester.

So she went to the B's. It seemed that Jeckel Island had been sold again. This time to something called TLC Ltd. There was no address. Just a handwritten note that said "Refer all inquiries to 381-1445. Ask for Furn." There wasn't even an area code.

Linka jotted down the company name and the number. She put the file back just where she had found it. Then she closed the drawer carefully.

Linka left the courthouse and looked for a pay phone. She dropped in a handful of change and dialed. She had a hunch it was a Pinchester number.

And she was right. High up in the one of the city's sleekest office towers, on a dressing table cluttered with bottles of nail

148

polish and tubes of lipstick, a pink princess telephone rang. After several rings a woman's voice answered.

"Hello?" she said.

"Is Furn there?" asked Linka.

"Furn? No. There's no Furn here."

"Then who am I speaking to?" asked Linka.

"You are speaking to Clareen Plagiste. I am Tucka Mertslin's executive assistant. This is a private line, and you obviously have the wrong number!"

"I'm afraid it's not quite so obvious to me," said Linka. Then she hung up.

Chapter 37
GONE WITH THE WIND

A brisk wind blew down the main street of the rose market, swirling clouds of red and pink rose petals along the sidewalk.

"Look at that!" said Hermux. "Now, that would make a nice picture."

But Terfle wasn't interested in atmospheric effects. She was on the lookout for the young squirrel. Hermux was too. But the wind was warm and fragrant, and it was such an ideal spring afternoon that Hermux couldn't entirely ignore it. Any more than he couldn't ignore the feeling of pride he had in Terfle's accomplishments as both an artist and a detective.

"You're doing a wonderful job," he told her. "That was first-class work comparing those three pictures."

Terfle felt that congratulations, while always welcome, were, in this particular case, premature. But she was glad that he had noticed. Appreciation made her work much easier. She was anxious to meet the young squirrel face-to-face and draw him from life.

"All right," said Hermux. "Here we are. Let's be very quiet."

Terfle didn't say a word. She seldom did. She turned to a fresh page in her sketchbook and checked the point of her pencil. She was ready.

The door to the old clocktower was pulled closed but still unlocked. Hermux opened it very carefully and was closing it behind them just as carefully when the wind caught it and slammed it shut with a crash. The sound echoed up and down the tower.

"So much for surprise," whispered Hermux.

Overhead there were sounds of movement. Someone was coming down. Hermux tiptoed back into the deep shadows beneath the stairs. He waited until he heard the footsteps reach the last landing. Then he stepped out and stood at the base of the staircase, blocking the door.

"Don't be scared," he said. "I just want to talk to you."

Halfway down the last flight of steps the young squirrel paused. He wore a backpack now and held the bedrolls against his chest.

Hermux tried to reassure him. "Nobody wants to hurt you—"

And that's when he charged. Squirrels have a significant advantage over mice when it comes to weight. And this squirrel was wearing a fully loaded backpack. The bedroll hit Hermux squarely in the chest. Fortunately for Hermux, it missed the Sport-a-Pet, or it might have broken his ribs. As it was, the impact knocked the wind out of Hermux and knocked Hermux off his feet.

"Oooof!" Hermux managed to say shortly before he landed flat on his back on the floor while the angry young squirrel raced right out the door.

"He's a hard one to talk to," said Hermux, struggling simultaneously to sit up and to breathe again. "Are you okay?" He inspected Terfle and the Sport-a-Pet for damage. He was relieved to find Terfle somewhat shaken but intact. "This Sport-a-Pet really does stand up to punishment."

Terfle nodded dreamily. Her heart was pounding, but not because she had narrowly escaped injury. As Hermux was flying through the air, she had managed, by acting quickly and keeping her wits about her, to get a good look at the young squirrel. For one split second she saw him clearly silhouetted against the bright doorway. He had spiky fur, a strong nose, and a bold, jutting chin. He looked just like her drawing. He looked like a young bandit. Terfle was smitten!

Hermux had regained his feet by then. He staggered out the door and started down the street after the squirrel. Slowly and painfully he began to jog.

The young squirrel was younger and naturally fast on his feet. But he was carrying a lot of extra weight. Hermux spotted him two blocks ahead. He veered around a corner and disappeared. When Hermux reached the spot, he found an alley that led back to the old docks behind the rose market. Hermux scanned the docks in both directions, but there was no sign of the young squirrel.

"Now what?" he asked Terfle. He noticed several breaks in the dock's railing. He investigated the first and discovered a rickety ladder nailed to the old pilings. The ladder led down to the water and a small landing. Tied up to it was a small, empty open boat.

He checked the next break and found a ladder there too, leading to another old, beat-up rowboat. At its oars sat the squirrel. He was just pushing off from the landing. He turned the rowboat and began to row.

Hermux yelled, "Stop! Don't go out there! It's dangerous!"

The squirrel looked up. Seeing Hermux, he began to row harder.

Hermux yelled louder. *"Stay away from the island! There are bees out there! Mutant bees! And guards with guns! Come back!"*

The wind took the words right out of his mouth, broke them into meaningless bits of sound, and scattered them across the bay. But Hermux was not ready to give up. He ran back to the first ladder, climbed into the boat, and untied it. Looking out at the choppy water, he saw that the squirrel had set a course directly for Jeckel Island.

"Batten down your hatches!" he told Terfle. He pushed the boat away from the landing and reached for the oars. But to his surprise there weren't any. It wasn't a rowboat. It was a sailboat. There was a small mast in the center and a boom that ran to the stern. A rope ran up the mast. Hermux grabbed it and pulled. To his delight a sail rose from the boom. He put his weight into it and hoisted it all the way to the top. He tied it off, and they were under way. As the boat emerged from the shelter of the dock, the sail caught the wind with a sharp snap. The boat leapt forward in the water, nearly throwing Hermux overboard. He scrambled to the back and grabbed the tiller with both hands. The wind whipped at his whiskers. It was an exhilarating feeling.

Then Hermux realized something. He didn't really know how to sail.

Chapter 38
S.O.S. (SINK OR SWIM)

"I may have made a mistake," Hermux told Terfle. There was no response. When he looked down to check on her, he saw that the curtains on the Sport-a-Pet were drawn tight. "I hope they're waterproof," he thought. And then, as though in answer to his query, a wave broke against the bow and drenched him. Water dripped from the fur on his chin and ran down his neck beneath his collar. Hermux's teeth began to chatter. He clamped them tight, and then ducked as the wind shifted suddenly and the boom swung to the other side. The sail cracked. The mast creaked. And the boat lurched. Hermux hung on, wrapping his tail around the tiller for good measure.

Ahead of them the squirrel continued to row at a fierce pace. But the sailboat was moving so much faster that it quickly overtook him. It then became apparent to Hermux that sailboats had a very serious design flaw—they did not have brakes. If he couldn't slow the boat soon or force it to change course, he would surely ram the rowboat from behind, which would be a certain catastrophe. He could see that the squirrel was not wearing a life jacket. For that matter, neither was he.

Hermux whispered a prayer. He leaned all his weight into

the tiller and the sailboat veered slightly to the left. The young squirrel stopped rowing briefly and watched the sailboat pass by. Hermux released one hand from the tiller just long enough to wave. Then he was gone from view.

Hermux could see Jeckel Island, looming closer. He could make out the dock and the ferry and beyond that a stretch of inviting, sandy beach. The problem was that now the sailboat was no longer headed toward the island. It was caught in the wind and the current. It was straight on course to the open sea.

Even to an inexperienced sailor like Hermux, that seemed like a very bad idea.

He remembered tales of shipwrecked sailors in their lifeboats, surrounded by water but dying of thirst. It would be an unpleasant way to die. And Linka might never know what happened to him. And then there was Terfle to consider. It was unfair that her life should end just as her career in art seemed to be taking off.

"No!" said Hermux with determination. "I shall not let that happen."

Despite the exhaustion in his arms and back, he pulled against the tiller. Little by little the boat changed direction until Hermux was able to line up the bow with the center of the beach. He kept his eyes on the band of solid, sunlit sand. He ignored the choppy waves ahead. He ignored the slosh of water on his feet. He ignored the icy cramps in his hands and the queasy feeling in his stomach and the mournful whistle of wind in his ears. He kept his mind focused entirely on the beach and visualized the boat coming in for a smooth, safe landing.

The landing did not turn out quite like he imagined. The boat hit the island with such momentum that it was driven ten feet up onto the beach. When it finally stopped, Hermux didn't.

Luckily, he missed the mast. He flipped over the bow and som-ersaulted onto the sand, landing more or less in a sitting posi-tion. He was still rubbing sand from his eyes when Hanger and Skuhl arrived.

"Put your hands in the air," said Hanger. "And don't make a move!"

Chapter 39
HOLE IN THE WALL

Hands over his head, Hermux marched up the flagstone walk toward the old farmhouse. He recognized it from Primm's photograph. Behind him came Hanger and Skuhl with their guns drawn.

"I say we should shoot him right now!" Hanger was itching to fire his new pistol. "Wollar said to shoot intruders on sight."

"Right," said Skuhl wearily. "But I'm just saying that we ought to make sure he qualifies as an intruder *before* we shoot him."

"Excuse me for interrupting," Hermux said over his shoulder. "But the gentleman's right. You ought to be sure first. And I can assure you that I'm *not* an intruder. I'm a sailor. A shipwrecked sailor, to be specific. You're not supposed to shoot me. You're supposed to give me warm blankets and hot chocolate." At least that was what he wanted. He wasn't sure what Terfle wanted, and he didn't want to draw attention to her by asking.

"You're on private property, buster! We'll do whatever we want to."

"I wasn't on private property until my boat crashed and threw me off!"

Skuhl thought that over. "He's got a point there."

But Hanger was not so easily swayed. "Don't get technical with us. We're the law here! You do what we tell you!"

"I did do what you told me. I put my hands in the air, and now you want to shoot me. It doesn't seem fair."

"The boss decides what's fair," said Hanger. "I'll go tell him we got an intruder right now. Put him in the house, Skuhl, and keep an eye on him." He started off in the direction of the barn. "And when I get back, then maybe we'll shoot you."

When he was out of earshot, Hermux spoke. "Your partner seems a little trigger-happy."

"Naw! He's just excited," Skuhl said. "We only got our guns this morning, and we haven't had a chance to use 'em yet." He poked Hermux in the back with his pistol. "Up the stairs."

"You're trained in gun safety, aren't you?" Hermux asked nervously.

"On-the-job training. Now get inside."

Skuhl ushered Hermux through the front door and into the living room. The mention of hot chocolate had made Skuhl think about food. His lunch bag was waiting in the refrigerator in the kitchen. He had packed a nut salad sandwich that morning. Now it was late afternoon, and he still hadn't eaten. First it was the hole in the garden. Then Wollar's cousin arrived and made a lot of ridiculous fuss about her cabin. And finally, to top it all off, there was the shipwrecked mouse. Regardless of what Hanger said, the mouse did not look like much of a threat to Skuhl. "I'll be right back," he said sternly. "You're going to wait here until I get back. And you're not going to move a muscle, understand?

Because you don't want to see me mad." To make his point, he pointed his gun at Hermux. "I've got something I've got to do."

As soon as he left, Hermux examined the room, looking for something to use as a weapon. Except for a wooden crate with a tablecloth over it, there was nothing unusual. There was a fireplace, but no poker. There were bookshelves, but no heavy books. Hermux went back to the crate. He pulled the tablecloth aside.

"A gym set," he said. "Maybe it's got barbells!"

He lifted the crate's lid. He took one look inside and quickly slammed the lid back down.

"Did you see what I saw?" he whispered.

Terfle, who by now had opened her curtains, nodded.

"There's a dead body in there!" he said. "These people are crazy! Let's get out of here!"

Hermux started for the front door. Then he had second thoughts. The front door led to the porch. The porch led to the steps. The steps led down to the empty lawn. The lawn led to the beach. He would make a perfect target all the way back to the boat. And then what? He still couldn't sail it.

There had to be another way out.

Two more doors opened off the living room. Hermux ran to the first and pulled it open. It was a closet. And not a tidy one. Everything was in a jumble. But even if he had wanted to, there was no time to organize it now. Hermux heard Skuhl returning and ran to the second door. He opened it and plunged inside, pulling the door closed after him. The first thing he noticed was that it was dark. The second thing he noticed was that the floor was not where he expected it to be. He was tumbling head over heels down a flight of stairs. He did two flips and a half twist and landed on his back in what felt like a pile of laundry. Nothing broke.

"I'm getting pretty good at this," he said. Then he felt for the steps and knocked on wood. "Sorry, Terfle! Looks like we've found the cellar. Are you okay?"

She answered with a faint tap of her bell.

"When we get home, I'm going to write a letter to the people at Sport-a-Pet. I'm very impressed."

Terfle was impressed too.

Upstairs the sound of footsteps reminded Hermux that getting home might not be a simple affair. The footsteps raced around the living room and exited toward the entry hall. The front door opened and slammed shut again. Skuhl had gone outside to look for him.

The cellar was dimly lit. Hermux followed the light to its source in a small window over a utility sink. Unfortunately, the window was barred. Except for the stairs there appeared to be no way out. Going back upstairs was not an appealing thought. And the angry sounds of Skuhl's return made it even less so.

"We have to hide," Hermux told Terfle. His nose detected a trace of something foreign in the air. Floating somewhere between the pungent smell of damp cement and the sour smell of dirty laundry was a hint of earth. In times of danger the smell of earth was instinctively the smell of safe haven. Hermux fled toward it without thinking. It seemed to come from behind a rack of shelves. He scrabbled toward them, trying to squeeze himself between the shelves. But the space was too narrow.

Upstairs the closet door in the living room was opened and shut with a curse. Skuhl's footsteps approached the cellar door.

Hermux panicked. As he grabbed the shelves and pulled, the cellar door opened.

"I know you're down there!" Skuhl shouted. "Come out with your hands up, and there won't be any shooting!"

Hermux edged himself behind the shelves and groped along the wall. He found more than he had dared to hope for. Chiseled in the cellar's cement wall was a rough hole. It was the size and shape that moles prefer. But it would make a perfectly acceptable hiding place for a mouse and a ladybug.

"You're making me mad!" Skuhl warned. Hermux heard him cock his pistol. "All right, you asked for it. I'm coming down."

Hermux crawled inside the hole and tugged the shelves back into place with hardly a sound. It had been nearly dark in the basement. It was totally dark in the hole.

"We'll have to stay here for a little while," he whispered. He had no idea how long. They might have to hide there for days. And what if the guards locked the cellar door and went away? How long could they hold out without food? Linka would never guess where they were. No one would. Hermux imagined his and Terfle's mummified bodies being discovered years in the future. Nobody would even know who they were.

"I'm sorry, Terfle. I got us out of the frying pan, but we may have landed in the fire."

Skuhl was coming down the steps now. Hermux drew back farther into the hole, expecting, but not finding, its end. He cautiously extended a paw into empty space. It did not appear to be a hole after all, but a tunnel. And from the hint of freshness in the air, it was a tunnel that led outdoors. Concentrating all his attention on the tingling tips of his whiskers, Hermux began to crawl forward. He made it perhaps ten feet before something

161

soft touched his face. He stopped, his heart pounding wildly. Cautiously he reached out a hand. Then he breathed a sigh of relief. It was only string. Lengths of string hung down from the ceiling. Hermux tugged at one. It was surprising strong for string. And it was sticky too.

Chapter 40
BEE IN HER BONNET

Killium directed Tucka's attention to the large, full-color poster that hung over his desk in the laboratory. "As you can see, the social bees, and that includes the honeybees, organize themselves into three distinct castes." The poster was organized into a pyramid. At the top was a single bee, larger than all the others. "The queen is the most important."

"Naturally," Tucka concurred.

"The queen is a super-female. She rules the hive. She is cared for around the clock by the worker bees and fed a special diet of royal jelly. It's one of the rarest and most expensive foods on earth."

"Yummy!" said Tucka. She pictured herself reclining on a cushion, surrounded by attentive employees, while she slathered royal jelly on a slice of toast.

"You'll notice the queen's unique size and shape. Narrow waist and full, rounded hips."

Tucka ran an appreciative hand over her own hip. "They're beautiful creatures."

"Below the queen are the drones. The males. As you can see, their bodies are larger and hairier than the female workers."

"Nice!" said Tucka. "I like them!"

"The males have neither pollen baskets nor wax glands because they don't do any work."

"Big surprise!" said Tucka.

"Then below the drones are the workers. The normal females. And the most numerous. They keep the hive running."

"I don't need to know about them," Tucka said. "Let's hear more about the drones."

"There's not much to say. They compete to mate with the queen and then they die."

"Well, I suppose that's only natural," sighed Tucka. An image came to her of Reezor Bleesom laid out in a rose-covered coffin. He was smiling.

Tucka caught her reflection in the shade of the chrome desk lamp. Her lips were positively sagging. "Let's move on to the Luscious Lip-Fix."

"I think we might want to wait a day or so," Killium recommended. "I'm concerned about your body developing a chemical dependency on the bee venom."

"Don't be ridiculous," said Tucka, but her lips *were* beginning to itch a little. "Besides, the whole point of beauty products is dependency. Let's do it!"

"I imagine that first you want to see the process I use for transforming a normal larva into a killer bee?"

"Wrong," Tucka responded. She plopped herself down in Killium's chair, pressed her mouth to the Lip-Fix, and pulled the strap over her head. "Hit me!" she mumbled, looking up at Killium with heavy eyes.

Killium disappeared for a moment and returned with a single bee trapped in a test tube. He opened the Lip-Fix, upended the tube, and dropped the bee in place. He closed the lid and flipped the switch.

Tucka closed her eyes and waited.

Moments later, a shriek shattered the quiet in the lab. Tucka ripped off the strap and pushed her chair back. She fanned her lips. "Oh, mama!" she gasped. "That's hot!"

The door to the lab burst open, and Hanger rushed in. He dropped into his shooting stance. His gun was drawn and pointed at Killium and Tucka.

"What are you doing?" asked Tucka. "Get out of here!"

"I heard a scream," Hanger tried to explain.

"You'll hear another one if you don't get out this instant!"

Hanger looked to Killium, who nodded.

"But—" he tried again to explain.

"Out!" Tucka said.

Hanger holstered his pistol and left. He was confused. He had been excited to tell Dr. Wollar the important news about the intruder. Now what were they supposed to do with the mouse? And what was Wollar's cousin screaming about, anyway? It looked like Wollar had slapped her in the mouth. But it sure hadn't shut her up.

As he neared the main building, he saw Skuhl running toward him, waving his arms frantically. Hanger hurried to meet him.

"Did you tell him?" Skuhl sputtered. He pressed his paw against his side and panted. He was completely winded.

"No!" complained Hanger. "He didn't even give me a chance!"

"Thank goodness for that!"

"What's wrong?"

"The mouse escaped."

"How?"

"I don't know. One minute he was there. Then he was gone. He's tricky!"

Hanger drew his gun again. "Where did he go?"

"The boat's still there. I checked. And the dock's clear."

"Then he must be in the woods! Let's go!"

Chapter 41
TUNNEL VISION

Hermux realized that the sticky string wasn't string at all. The words *black widow* flashed in his mind like a neon sign while images of Big Mama's ice-pick fangs danced around him in the dark. Hermux gagged on a mouthful of spiderweb. He spit it out and started crawling as fast as he could.

"Fasten your seat belt, Terfle! It's going to be a bumpy ride!"

Terfle's seat belt had been fastened for some time. And her sketchbook and pencil were carefully stowed. As he scurried ahead, Hermux tried to remember which spiders lived in holes and crevices; which ones ate their victims on the spot; which ones stored them away for a rainy day; and which ones wove the big webs to catch their prey. It was the last that most worried him.

When the tunnel made a right turn, Hermux ran headfirst into the wall. After that he had to slow and use one paw to feel ahead of him. It was a good thing because it wasn't long before he encountered the remains of a web that had been stretched across the tunnel. One side had been torn away. Hermux crept around the trap and edged his way forward, warier than ever. Just beyond the web the tunnel branched in two.

"What do you think?" he whispered. "The left one or the right?"

Then they heard the faintest of noises. From the tunnel on the right came the stealthy skittering of many feet. Terfle thumped her bell in alarm.

Hermux went left. He raced through the tunnel, scraping his knuckles and banging his head. But the end of the tunnel was soon in sight. With enough light to see, Hermux began to pick up speed.

As he reached his top speed, he ran smack into a web. It was impossible to see. Wall-to-wall, freshly spun, extra-sticky, and tight as a drum. Hermux's momentum carried him forward, stretching the web nearly eight feet before it snapped like a trampoline and catapulted him right back down the tunnel again. As he hurtled through space, Hermux caught sight of a bulky blob lurching hungrily toward him on spindly legs. Too many legs. Too many eyes. And way too many fangs. Hermux braced himself for the impact and worse. Then the web sprang back. And Hermux went with it.

"Prepare for orbit!" he shouted to Terfle. As the web began to slow, Hermux's feet sought traction. He clawed the dirt and pumped his legs with all the strength he had. The web stretched to the max. Closer and closer it came to breaking. For a tantalizing second Hermux saw daylight. Freedom was mere feet away. The spider silk stretched, but it would not break. Behind him the spider lumbered nearer. Frantic with fear, Hermux began to bite at the web. His sharp teeth snapped cord after cord until suddenly Hermux popped free and shot out of the tunnel like a Ping-Pong ball from an airgun. He tumbled to a stop at the edge of a quiet stream. As he sat there dazed, the spider reached the tunnel's entrance. Then it prepared to spring.

168

"Over here!" a voice shouted from nearby upstream. "I heard him yell!"

"I heard him too!" someone answered.

It was Hanger and Skuhl.

Hermux struggled to his feet. The spider quietly withdrew into the safety of the tunnel.

"You work your way downstream," Hanger yelled. "I'll work my way up."

Hermux and Terfle were caught in the middle.

Chapter 42
HITTING THE SAUCE

Killium removed a glass vial from the refrigerator and filled the hypodermic syringe. "Then I inject the serum into the larva of the bee. I cover it with wax. And voilà! Two weeks later—a killer bee!"

"What's in the serum?" asked Tucka.

"Oh, a little of this and a little of that. It's very technical."

"Try me," said Tucka.

Killium reluctantly handed her the bottle. Tucka held it up to the light. Then she brought it in very close and peered at the label, which was covered with tiny letters and numbers.

"That's the formula," said Killium.

"I can see that." She began reading. After a minute she stopped. "It's pretty complicated."

"I tried to tell you. Genetic engineering isn't simple."

Tucka studied the label again. Then, using a razor-sharp claw, she carefully sliced through it and peeled it from the bottle. Beneath it was another label. A very familiar label.

"Oh, my!" she said in mock surprise. "What in the world could this be?"

She read it out loud.

Chaleeta's Five-Alarm Chili Pepper Sauce

Avoid contact with eyes.

She ran a fingertip over her newly luscious lips. "Well, Chaleeta!" she said. "You pack quite a wallop!" Her lips still throbbed, but it was a feeling she was starting to like. "Dr. Wollar, I'm beginning to think that you're a little twisted."

"I like to think of myself as *original*," Killium countered. "Unexpected results demand unorthodox methods."

"I couldn't agree more," said Tucka. "And that's why we make such a good pair. By the way, I spoke to Moozella Corkin this morning before I left Pinchester. She told me that now Reezor has decided to kick off his Bed of Roses party with a victory tour of his new rose garden. The roses are supposed to be in full bloom on Saturday, and he intends to rub them in my face. He actually plans to ride in a parade float while the rest of us follow along on foot."

"The little weasel!"

"Exactly what I said. Oh, and I called my car dealer. He's got a dandy little Frugatti 260T convertible in the showroom. He says it's fast as lightning."

"It is?" Killium began to drool.

"Pricey too."

"What did you tell him?"

"I said I'd call him after Reezor's party. Speaking of which, don't you have something you want to show me?"

Chapter 43
UP A TREE

Hermux had only seconds to react. The options for escape weren't good. One bank of the stream was too steep to scramble up. On the other the underbrush was too dense to squeeze through. At least too dense for a mouse with a penchant for donuts. And that left only the tunnel, which was definitely not a good idea.

Hermux snapped open the Sport-a-Pet's door.

"Fly for it!" he told Terfle. "If you can get to the mainland, tell Linka what happened!"

Terfle refused to leave him. They were in this together.

"All right," said Hermux. Hoping that the guards wouldn't shoot somebody who was ready to surrender, he raised his hands. When he did, he was surprised to feel something dangling right over his head. For one awful moment, it felt like a spiderweb.

But it wasn't sticky; it was rough and dry. It was a rope. Hermux grabbed hold of it and started to climb up. As he did, the rope began to move. Branches and leaves whipped by his face as Hermux felt himself being pulled straight up through the trees. Below him Hanger and Skuhl splashed ashore.

"Where'd he go?" Hanger shouted. "I know I heard him!"

"He didn't get by me!" claimed Skuhl. "He must have gotten away through the brush. What do we do?"

Hanger considered the situation. "We'll split up. You go back to the sailboat. I'll watch the ferry. There's only two ways off this island."

When the rope stopped moving, Hermux found himself hanging over a hole in the wooden floor of a big tree house.

"Where are we?" he whispered to Terfle. The rope ran through a pulley on the branch above them and from there to a hand winch that was bolted to the trunk. Hermux was astonished to find the young squirrel operating the winch. He was more astonished when the boy set the winch's brake and picked up a slingshot.

He aimed it right at Hermux. "Who are you?" he demanded. "And why are you following me?"

"We're not following you," Hermux tried to explain. He couldn't tell if the squirrel was angry or scared.

"Yes, you are. You've been following me all day. Are you a cop?"

"A cop? No! I'm a watchmaker." Hermux's palms were sweating, and he felt himself beginning to slip.

"I don't believe you."

"I can show you my card if you'll just help me down. I need to get down fast!"

"Fine!" the squirrel said. He reached for the brake on the winch.

"No!" Hermux said. "Not that fast. Please!"

Terfle leapt from the Sport-a-Pet and flew right at the squirrel, buzzing around his head like an electron. She may have had a terrific crush on the young squirrel, but that didn't give him the right to put Hermux in danger.

"What is that? And what's it doing?" The squirrel swatted wildly with both hands.

"That's my friend Terfle," said Hermux.

"Does it sting?"

"Not unless I tell her to. Get me down from here, and I'll call her off!"

"Okay! Okay! Just make her stop. I don't like bugs."

Terfle relented while the squirrel pulled Hermux to safety.

"Thank you," said Hermux. As soon as he was on solid wood, he reached for the slingshot and confiscated it. "I don't think you'll need this."

"Give it back!" the squirrel said.

"After the introductions," said Hermux. "By the way, I'm Hermux Tantamoq. And this my associate Terfle." She made a graceful landing on Hermux's outstretched hand. "Terfle is a ladybug."

Terfle curtsied and peered eagerly up at the young squirrel.

"Ladybugs don't sting!" the squirrel protested. "You lied."

"Not exactly," said Hermux. "Besides, Terfle is no ordinary ladybug. She drew a portrait of you, you know. It's really good. Everybody thinks so."

"Why'd she do that?" the squirrel asked. No one had ever drawn his picture. "And why are you following me? You lied about that too, didn't you. And why were those men chasing you?"

"Whoa!" said Hermux. "I've got a few questions for you first. To begin with, why did you drop us the rope?"

"They had guns. It wasn't fair."

"No, it wasn't," Hermux said. "Thanks for noticing. And thanks for saving our lives. We owe you."

Terfle, who had returned to Hermux's shoulder, nodded emphatically.

"Whatever," the squirrel said.

Hermux glanced around the tree house. It was one room, about eight by twelve feet, with a ramshackle roof, unfinished walls, and the access hole in the floor. There were windows that had once had glass and curtains that hung now in shreds. A kitchen counter of sorts was built against one wall. On it sat a bag of groceries half unpacked. Except for a tattered backpack and two old bedrolls, the rest of the tree house was bare.

"Who built this place?" Hermux asked.

"I don't know," said the squirrel. "My dad found it. He's got real sharp eyes. You can't see it from below."

"The older guy's your dad?" Hermux asked. That would explain a few things.

The squirrel nodded.

"Where is he?"

"I don't know!" The squirrel kicked angrily at one of the bedrolls. "He's gone. Why do *you* want to know?"

"Because this island isn't safe, especially for a boy on his own."

"I'm not on my own. I'm with my dad."

"I'm just telling you those men that were chasing us are dangerous. And the people they work for are even more dangerous. You shouldn't be out here."

"Where am I supposed the go? We were all set at the clocktower. You chased me out."

"I'm sorry. I didn't mean to. I just wanted to ask what you two were doing out at the Villa DeRosenquill."

"I don't know. Dad wandered out there, and I followed him.

He gets confused sometimes. They chased us off. People are mean to him."

"I'm sorry."

"You're sorry a lot, aren't you?" the squirrel said irritably. "Well, sorry doesn't help."

"I didn't mean to offend you," Hermux said. "What's your name?"

"Twigg."

"I'm really pleased to meet you, Twigg." Hermux offered his hand. "I hope we can be friends."

Uncertainly Twigg offered his, and they shook hands.

"Do you have a last name?" Hermux asked.

"No."

"Okay," said Hermux. "Just plain Twigg. It's a nice name. What's your dad's name?"

"Just Dad."

"I see."

Terfle had returned to the Sport-a-Pet to get her sketchbook. She had made a place for herself on the kitchen counter and was drawing Twigg's head with swift, sure strokes of her pencil.

"Would you like to see the drawing she made of you?" Hermux asked.

"Sure," Twigg said.

Hermux removed the drawing from his pocket, somewhat soggy and worse for wear, and began to unfold and smooth it out on the countertop. As he did, Twigg struggled to appear blasé, but finally lost patience and snatched it away.

"That's me!" he said. "Cool."

"I had it blown up," Hermux said. "She normally works in a smaller scale."

Twigg grew suspicious.

"If she's never seen me before, how did she draw my picture?"

"I described you to her from yesterday in the clocktower when you knocked me — When we met. Terfle is very creative."

"Can I have it?"

"You'll have to ask her," said Hermux.

Twigg turned to Terfle. "Can I have it?"

She ignored him and kept drawing.

"You might try 'please,'" Hermux suggested.

"Nobody's ever drawn my picture before," Twigg told Terfle. "Can I please have it?"

Terfle consented.

"Thank you," Twigg said unexpectedly. If Terfle could have blushed, she would have. Instead, she went back to her drawing. The late afternoon light poured through the tree house's single window, bathing Twigg's head and torso with golden light. It was a dramatic effect, and Terfle was concentrating hard and working quickly to capture it on paper before the light changed.

Twigg folded the drawing carefully and put it in his backpack. "Why were those guys chasing you, anyway?" he asked Hermux.

"I don't know. All I know is that these guards have guns now and they have orders to shoot."

"Why?"

"I don't know that either. But something funny is going on on this island."

"What happened to your boat?"

Hermux and Terfle looked at each other. Terfle waved at Twigg and pointed toward the patch of light.

"We left it on the beach," Hermux said. "I think Terfle wants you to get back into the light and hold still."

"Oh," said Twigg. He returned to his place and stood up very straight and stiff.

"Try to act normal," said Hermux. "Terfle is specializing in realistic drawing."

"Okay," said Twigg. He tried to relax, but looked even stiffer. "So you're really not a cop?"

Hermux smiled. "No. I really am a watchmaker. But I do some detective work on the side. I'm working on a case now."

"Am I part of it?" Twigg tried to hold his pose and not move lips much when he spoke.

"Actually, I'm investigating a missing squirrel. His family used to own this island."

"They owned a whole island?"

"They're very rich."

"Lucky squirrels!" said Twigg.

"Maybe," replied Hermux.

Terfle rapped her pencil on the counter. She sounded irritated.

"We should stop talking until she's finished," Hermux suggested.

"Okay by me."

While Terfle drew, Hermux observed the young squirrel. Without his overcoat he looked less like a gangster and more like an ordinary boy, although one who had led a difficult life. He was maybe twelve years old. His clothes were nearly worn through. And his fur looked as though it had never been washed or brushed even once. But despite the neglect he carried himself proudly. His eyes were alert and intelligent. Terfle was right. His resemblance to the young Buddlin DeRosenquill in the photograph was uncanny. But as Hermux watched him, and as he settled into his pose, the angry lines in his face faded. A more thoughtful, almost whimsical, expression took their place. He looked less and less like Buddlin and more and more like Plank.

Hermux considered the possibility that Twigg could be Plank's son. He was about the right age. His father seemed to have known something about Jeckel Island. And he knew about the tree house. He must have known about the Jeckel roses that Twigg was picking and selling in town.

"And speaking of town," Hermux said suddenly. "We've got to get going! Linka has no idea where we are. She must be worried."

Terfle finished her drawing, closed her sketchbook, and prepared to leave.

"Can I see it?" Twigg asked.

She gave him her sketchbook. Hermux gave him his magnifier and showed him how to hold it in his eye and keep the sketchbook at just the right distance.

"Wow!" Twigg said when his portrait came into focus. "That's really me, isn't it? I'm handsome."

"I suppose you are," said Hermux. "But I think it depends on the viewer. Terfle certainly thinks so."

"Thank you, Terfle," said Twigg. "Thank you very much." Hermux was right. She was no ordinary bug.

Chapter 44
Table for Four

Twigg didn't want to leave the tree house. He was worried about his father. Sometimes his father had restless spells. It was a restless spell that had brought them to Thorny End. But once they were there, father had gotten depressed. He retreated to his bedroll in the clocktower and hardly spoke or ate for days. Then the restlessness returned with a vengeance. In a state of wild excitement he showed Twigg the tree house and announced big plans for fixing it up and furnishing it and making it their permanent home—something that Twigg had dreamed of having for as long as he could remember.

"Then he disappeared," Twigg told them. "He's done that before, but he always comes back. I think he'll come here, and I've got to be here when he does. He may crash again. I need to take care of him."

It took a lot to convince Twigg to return with them. It took the promise of a hot meal, the prospect of spending more time with Terfle, and, finally, the offer of Linka's plane to mount an airborne search of the area for his father. The plane wasn't really his to offer, but Hermux couldn't imagine Linka saying no, once she heard the whole story.

Together they decided that the wisest and most practical way to get back to the mainland was to go with Twigg in his rowboat. Twigg admitted that it wasn't really his rowboat. But it had looked deserted when he and his father had found it. And so far no one had seemed to notice that it was being used.

Twilight was falling as they slipped away from the island. Twigg had made the trip many times before. He rowed while Hermux and Terfle sat at the stern. The air was still. The water was calm. The sun was setting in a cloudless sky. Terfle worked on a number of quick studies of Twigg at the oars. This was exactly the opportunity she had been waiting for. As soon as she returned to Pinchester, she intended show Mirrin the drawings and ask for her help in developing one of them into an oil painting. Hermux was not so industrious. After the day they had had, he was just glad to be alive.

They tied up at the wharf and went to look for Linka. Hermux decided that the inn was the most likely place she would wait. And he was right. They found her in the dining room seated by a window. When she saw Hermux, she nearly pushed her chair over in her excitement.

"I'm so glad to see you!" she said. "I was starting to worry." She threw her arms around Hermux and gave him a squeeze, pressing the Sport-a-Pet right against the sorest part of his ribs.

He was glad to see her too, but it still hurt. "Ow!" he said against his will.

"What's wrong?" asked Linka.

There was a lot to tell her. But first there were introductions to make. And there was food to order. They were all starving.

Twigg had never eaten in a restaurant. And although he could hold his own against street bullies twice his size and he was

181

not afraid of water or heights or strange towns or dark places, he found himself feeling a little intimidated by cloth napkins and menus and way too much silverware.

Linka, who was known for her own courage and spunkiness, was quite taken by Twigg's. "Do you like walnuts?" she asked him.

Twigg nodded. What squirrel doesn't?

"Then you know what sounds good to me?" she said. "The walnut loaf with baby carrots. Carrots are very good this time of year. That's what I'm having. What about you?"

"Me too," said Twigg. He closed his menu, looking very relieved.

There wasn't much on the menu to suit a ladybug. But Terfle settled for a child's portion of silverfish pâté with some crumbs of toast. Hermux ordered a blue cheese cornburger and crispy fries. And soon the entire table was munching contentedly while questions were asked and answered.

Linka told the story of tracing Tucka's ownership of the island.

Hermux told the story of finding Twigg at the clocktower.

"I'm sorry about knocking you down," Twigg said. "I thought you were a cop or somebody from welfare."

"Forget it," Hermux told him. "We're more than even." He turned to Linka. "This brave young man saved Terfle and me from who-knows-what at the hands of those guards."

"What guards?" asked Linka.

"The ones who captured us when I wrecked the sailboat on the island."

"What sailboat? You don't know how to sail!"

"I know that now. But I'd like to learn. It was fun there for a while."

"Hermux, I have a feeling you're not telling me everything."

"I'll tell you later," he said. He caught her eye and tipped his head imperceptibly toward Twigg. "Why don't you tell Twigg about some of the rescue missions you've flown?"

"Yeah!" Twigg chimed in. "I'd like to hear!"

Linka laughed. "Well, young man, after years of flying them, one thing I've learned is that I need a clear head to do it. And that means a good night's sleep. It's time for us to head home."

Sleep sounded good to Hermux.

"You can fly back to Pinchester with us," Hermux told Twigg. "You'll be safe there, and we'll come back here first thing tomorrow morning."

"No," Twigg said. "I'm going back to the island."

"You can't go back there," said Hermux. "You heard! It's dangerous. I didn't even tell you about the killer bees!"

"What bees?"

"Or the spider."

"What spider?"

"Never mind! You're not going back."

But Twigg, who could be very brave, could also be very stubborn. He would not leave Thorny End until his father was found.

It was Linka who proposed a solution.

"We'll all stay," she said. "It will save us a roundtrip anyway. I've got sleeping bags in the plane. And a camp stove and a coffeepot. Besides, I want to see this tree house!"

Chapter 45

ROCK~A~BYE BABY

Hermux strung a piece of twine across the center of the tree house and draped a blanket over it for Linka's privacy. She and Terfle were sleeping on one side. He and Twigg on the other.

"Everyone comfortable?" Linka asked.

"Yes," answered Hermux and Twigg.

Hermux zipped his sleeping bag to the top. The night had cooled considerably.

"All right then," said Linka. "Sweet dreams, all of you!" She crawled into her sleeping bag and blew out the candle. The tree house was plunged into darkness. Not the sort of half darkness you see in towns and suburbs. But real darkness. A slight wind rustled the leaves, and the tree house creaked and swayed ever so gently, like a boat anchored in a sheltered cove. Despite the dangers that he knew lurked on the island, Hermux felt remarkably safe and secure in their treetop hideaway. He snuggled down into his bag until only his ears and nose stuck out.

"Thank you," he thought, "for narrow escapes. Particularly the escape part. Thank you for Terfle's sharp eye. Thank you for family photos and detective agencies and sailboats and secret tunnels. And thank you especially for the excellent workmanship of all the folks at the Sport-a-Pet company. I hate to think what would have happened without them." When it came to the DeRosenquill family, he couldn't think what to say. He left it with, "Thank you for family ties."

Then he let the day go and drifted off contentedly toward sleep. He was almost gone when a plaintive voice broke the quiet.

"I can't sleep."

It was Twigg.

"What's wrong?" Hermux forced himself awake.

"I don't know. Everything is whirling around. I can't stop thinking."

"Did you try counting grasshoppers?" Hermux asked. It often worked for him.

"Sometimes Dad reads to me," Twigg said.

"What do you have?"

"The Runaway Squirrel."

That woke Hermux up. He had totally forgotten. Linka relit the candle. Soon they were gathered around Twigg. Terfle took the opportunity to join Twigg in his sleeping bag. She nestled down next to him and waited eagerly for Hermux to begin.

Hermux held the book up to the candle. He opened it to the title page and found an inscription.

HAPPY BIRTHDAY, PLANK!

LOVE,
PRIMM

Hermux's heart skipped a beat. He held the book out for Linka to see. And then he began to read.

Before he had finished the first chapter, Twigg's eyes grew

185

heavy. By the end of the second they were closed. And by the third both he and Terfle were snoring lightly.

Linka stole away to the far side of the tree house and beckoned Hermux to follow.

"Well, that cinches it, don't you think?" she whispered. "Twigg's father is definitely Plank DeRosenquill. Now we've just got to find him."

"There may be one problem," Hermux said sadly. He told her about his gruesome discovery in the crate in the living room of the institute. "What if it's him?"

Linka's first thought was Twigg. "The poor little guy! What'll we do?"

"I don't know," said Hermux.

"We have to tell Androse and Primm."

"Do we?" Hermux remembered their last meeting with Androse. "I'm not sure."

"Hermux!" Linka hissed. "Wake up!"

Hermux woke with a start. He was in a sleeping bag. In a tree house. On an island. It was the middle of the night.

"What is it?"

"I heard something."

"What?"

"I don't know. Let's find out!"

The moon had risen full, and a pale glow trickled through the canopy of leaves. Linka was already dressed. Hermux followed suit.

"Let's go," she whispered.

A trail of boards nailed to the tree's trunk formed a ladder of sorts. Linka had no trouble crawling down. Reluctantly Hermux followed. Once on the ground they stepped out of the tree's shadow and found themselves in a world transformed by moonlight.

From the distance came a metallic clang. And a cry.

"Sounds like someone's hurt," said Linka. "It coming from that way."

"The institute," said Hermux.

They followed the stream out of the forest toward the beach. Above the beach was a large field. The farmhouse stood at the edge of the field. They crept through the grass and hid in the shadows of an old arbor engulfed by a ghostly white rose. From behind the house came the unmistakable sounds of a struggle. A dark figure appeared, pushing a wheelbarrow into the garden. Something big and boxy was balanced on top of it. And from the looks of it, that something was heavy.

Hermux recognized it immediately. "It's the crate from the living room," he whispered.

"Who is it?"

"It looks like a mouse. I'll bet it's Wollar. He's the boss."

"What's he doing?"

As though in answer, the mouse tilted the wheelbarrow up. The crate slid off and disappeared into the earth with a crash.

"Finally!" the mouse muttered. He slumped on the wheelbarrow, clutching his chest and breathing heavily.

"He's burying it," whispered Hermux.

"Let's get out of here!"

"Nothing would give me greater pleasure."

They slipped away together as stealthily as they had come.

Chapter 47
MAIN DRAG

The sun was just coming up. Twigg and Terfle were still asleep. Terfle's head rested against Twigg's shoulder.

"They look sweet together," said Linka.

"She's always wanted an older brother," said Hermux. "I just hope he's a good influence."

"Should we wake them?"

"I hate to. I don't know if I'm ready to face Twigg. Besides, before we say anything, we need to be absolutely sure."

"Then what do we do?"

"It's time to go to the police."

They slipped out quietly, leaving a note behind.

> Dear Twigg & Terfle,
>
> We got up early and went to town to follow up on some important leads. We will be back soon. Until then stay in the tree house and stay out of sight.
>
> Hermux & Linka
>
> P.S. We took the rowboat.

The crossing was smooth. After watching Twigg handle the oars, Hermux rowed well enough, and they were soon tying up to the old wharf. They climbed up the ladder in time to see the ferry steaming in from Jeckel Island. They slipped down the dock and observed its arrival.

On board were two mice. One was a skinny guy in a natty brown suit. He was at the wheel.

"Do you think that's Wollar?" asked Linka.

"It must be."

"And who's *she*? She certainly doesn't look local."

She was a cheap-looking blonde in tight jeans and a low-cut sweatshirt. Even from a distance it was obvious that she had larger-than-usual lips.

When the ferry came to a stop, the blonde kissed the skinny mouse good-bye, then she gathered her purse and an overnight bag and stepped ashore. She waved gaily and then turned to walk toward Main Street. The ferry reversed its engine and returned toward Jeckel Island.

"Let's follow her," said Linka, "and see where she goes."

"Right," said Hermux.

The blonde ambled along Main Street at a leisurely pace. Moving at an equally leisurely pace, Hermux and Linka were never far behind. From time to time, the blonde stopped to inspect the contents of a shop window, and when she did, she checked her watch for the time. Hermux checked his as well. At exactly 9:16, according to Hermux's watch, which was extremely reliable as you might imagine, the blonde opened the door of Dockery's Frockery and disappeared inside.

Chapter 48
AWOL

Twigg was not the sort of squirrel who bounded out of bed in the morning. He was more the slow type—and a little bit grumpy if you really want to know the truth. He yawned noisily several times. He sat up and stretched. Then he crawled out of his sleeping bag and slowly, and very groggily, lumbered down the ladder, where he proceeded to dunk his head in the stream several times.

Terfle had already been up for some time. She had entertained herself, first by sketching Twigg sleeping, and then moving on to a series of detailed drawings of the tree house, which she found utterly charming in the morning light. She couldn't wait to show these to Glissin back at the theater. She was sure they would come in handy as ideas for set designs if Fluster Varmint ever mounted a revival of *The Runaway Squirrel.*

She was putting the finishing touches on a view of the window. With its missing panes and its faded scrap of curtain, it made a melancholy picture. She concentrated on capturing the mood and ignored the crude sounds of grunting, gargling, and gurgling that came from below. Hermux was certainly a more civilized companion in the morning.

She was pleasantly surprised, though, when Twigg reappeared through the hole in the floor and asked cheerfully, "Where is everybody? Have you had breakfast yet?"

She indicated that she hadn't.

"What do you eat in the morning?" he asked. "I like cereal myself."

Terfle did not. She had tried it once, but found it hopelessly bland. Hermux had left a tin of dried aphids for her on the counter. She pointed it out. Hermux had used it as a paperweight for his note.

"What's this?" asked Twigg when he saw the note.

As he read it, his face changed from cheerful to his more familiar scowl.

He read it again, this time aloud. "Why does everybody think they can give me orders? What if I don't want to stay here and wait?" He seemed to forget that staying in the tree house and waiting had been his idea to begin with. Not only had he forgotten it, but now the mere idea of waiting was humiliating. The tree house suddenly felt like a prison. He had to get out. "Let's eat," he said. "And then we'll go exploring. I want to see that tunnel!"

Chapter 49
CHANGING ROOM

Hermux and Linka waited. Ten minutes had gone by, and there was no sign of the blonde. Hermux sauntered past the storefront and glanced inside. Except for the salesclerk, the store appeared empty.

"Maybe I'd better go in and check," said Linka. She slipped on her sunglasses and wrapped a scarf around her head. She walked up to the store window and stood a moment eyeing one of the mannequins, which was dressed in a light summer dress of dotted swiss embroidered all over with giant strawberries. It had a big full skirt, puffy sleeves, and a giant bow on the collar. It was not quite her style.

Nevertheless, she stepped into the shop and asked the clerk breezily if it was available in her size. It was.

"I wonder if I could try it on?" Linka asked.

"You'll have to wait a moment," the clerk said. "The dressing room is occupied." She turned to face Linka and said in a whisper, "She's been in there quite a while. I hope she's not a shoplifter."

She had no sooner spoken than the door of the dressing room opened and a woman with astonishingly luscious red lips stepped out. However, it was not the blonde. This mouse was older and more sophisticated and decidedly brunette. It was Tucka Mertslin. She was dressed for a garden party. And she appeared to be in a hurry.

"Thank you, dear," she told the clerk as she swept toward the door. "But nothing fit."

As Tucka passed her, Linka held a sweater up to her face and pretended to read the label. Then she ran to the door and watched as Tucka stepped to the curb, put her fingers to her luscious lips, and gave a sharp whistle. Seconds later a limousine pulled up, and Tucka got in.

"Reezor Bleesom's place," she told the chauffeur. "And hurry! I don't want to miss a thing!"

Chapter 50
STICK BY ME

Twigg wasn't afraid of the dark. Neither was Terfle normally. But normally the dark didn't contain a large and obviously hungry spider. Terfle had seen too many nature magazines. She knew what spiders liked to eat—her. On her last ride through the tunnel she had been inside the Sport-a-Pet. At least that offered some protection. But for this trip they had left the Sport-a-Pet behind, and now here she was, riding bareback on Twigg's shoulder into the Tunnel of Death.

"This way you won't be all cooped up," Twigg had told her. "And you'll be able to see better. It'll be exciting." A little too exciting for Terfle. She had always heard that love made people do foolish things, but this was ridiculous.

On the other hand, there was something very romantic about it. The tunnel was even spookier by candlelight. Perched on Twigg's sturdy shoulder, Terfle felt like a character in a fairy tale. It reminded her of the story of the kindly woodsman who was sent by the old witch into the haunted mine to retrieve the golden shovel that could talk. Unlike some of the other tales that Hermux had read to her, this one had a happy ending. The

shovel turned out to be an enchanted princess. And the woodsman was really a handsome prince in disguise.

"Which way?" Twigg asked when they reached the intersection of the tunnels. When Terfle hesitated, he went left. "This one
looks good. We can come back and do the other."

"If we're lucky," thought Terfle.

"Look!" said Twigg. He held the candle higher. "There's a
door up ahead!"

Sure enough, the tunnel ended at a wooden door.

"And look. There's a poster on it. Can you read it?"

The poster was old and stained with moisture. The once gar-
ish colors had faded to pastels.

Plank DeRosenquill
presents
3 days of peace and love!
THE JECKEL ISLAND ROCK FESTIVAL

"I bet I can sell that for some real cash. It's vintage," Twigg
explained to Terfle. "That means it's worth more money. Ever
been to a rock festival?"

Terfle shook her head.

"Me neither. But someday I'm going!" He examined the poster more closely. "Except for the stains, it's in pretty good shape."

Twigg set the candle down and leaned his stick against the wall. Then he began to pry out the thumbtacks that held up the poster. The first one came easily. But the others were stuck hard and took some time. While he worked, Terfle kept a vigilant watch over his shoulder. The flickering candle made it difficult to see.

"Almost got it," Twigg said. "Are you okay?"

Suddenly she wasn't. Terfle watched spellbound as a pale strand of web emerged from the darkness. Weightless as smoke and nearly as transparent, it drifted past her. It floated down toward Twigg's walking stick and looped itself around. Then it tightened.

Terfle tried to warn Twigg. But she didn't have a bell.

Without warning the stick sprang away from the wall.

"Hey!" Twigg exclaimed.

Then the stick shot down the tunnel and vanished into the dark.

Just beyond the reach of the light something scuttled forward along the floor. Twigg and Terfle both saw it at once.

Twigg moved faster than he had ever moved in his life. He opened the door, jumped through it, slammed it shut, and blocked it with his body.

Meanwhile, when Terfle had seen the spider racing toward them like a big hairy cannonball on legs, she seemed to lose her grip on reality. She even lost her grip on Twigg. And so when he made his move, Terfle was left behind. Terfle found herself weightless, mometarily suspended in space before she plummeted to the floor. Twigg's candle had been knocked over and flared up. At the end of the tunnel sprawled a fat, hairy body. But there was no sign of Twigg.

The spider was getting to its feet. If she didn't want to be brunch, it was time for Terfle to take her leave. She opened her wings and started back the way she and Twigg had come.

On the other side of the door, Twigg faced the horrible realization that Terfle had been left behind. He hesitated for one moment. Just long enough to take his slingshot from his left rear pocket and load it with a smooth, round rock from his front right. He drew the slingshot to its maximum extension and kicked open the door.

The tunnel was silent and empty.

Then in the distance something moved. A shadow against shadows.

The shadow turned slowly then lurched forward, gathering speed as it came. Twigg pulled back the sling and braced himself. This was one shot he couldn't afford to miss.

Chapter 51
TICKET TO RIDE

The limousine pulled away, leaving Hermux and Linka standing on the sidewalk, gaping in astonishment.

"I think that pretty much sums it up," said Hermux, reading the license plate on the back of the vanishing limo, which said VANITY.

"I don't know," Linka mused. "I think RUTHLESS would work."

"Hadn't thought of that," Hermux admitted. "And what about HEARTLESS?"

"Nice. But too many letters."

"What do you think she was doing on the island? And why was she in disguise?"

"And why is she going to Reezor's party?"

"Free food?" Hermux suggested. "I know he's serving good donuts. But why on earth would he invite her? I'd be afraid to let her in my house."

"Maybe he's afraid not to." Linka grew more serious. "Do you think she knows about the body?"

"She might," said Hermux. "But if she did, I can't see her burying it in the rose garden. It doesn't seem safe."

Linka considered the various problems of secretly disposing of a body. "Maybe she thinks it's so obvious that no one would ever suspect."

"But they've got a boat," argued Hermux. "I think Tucka would dump the body at sea."

"Maybe they already tried that. The body washed up on the beach, remember? Maybe they took it out to sea and the tide brought it back."

"You're so smart," said Hermux admiringly. It was so much more fun being a detective when Linka was with him, he realized. It seemed easier too. "But that still leaves the big questions unanswered. Whose body is it? And why was he killed?"

As they spoke, they had begun walking. Now their steps quickened.

"It's time we talk to the police," said Hermux.

"We can tell them that Plank's gone missing."

"And we'll report the body on Jeckel Island. They can get a search warrant to dig it up."

Thorny End was not exactly the crime capital of the middle coast. Nevertheless, it boasted both a sheriff and a police department. They shared office space across the hall from the Records Office in the courthouse basement. Linka had noticed it the day before.

They also shared a desk sergeant, who was reading the morning paper as Hermux and Linka walked in. He looked up from it just long enough to size them up. "Upstairs," he said, and went back to reading.

"Excuse me?" said Hermux.

"Marriage licenses. Second floor. Third door on the right." The sergeant didn't bother looking up again.

"But we're not here to get married," said Hermux. "At least

200

not yet. We're still in the planning stages. We want to file a report."

"Two reports," added Linka.

Wearily the sergeant put the paper down. "I'm all ears!" he said.

"First we'd like to report a missing person," said Hermux. "Male, squirrel, mid-to-late thirties, wearing a—"

"Hold on there!" the sergeant broke in. "Is this county or city?"

"What difference does it make?" asked Linka. "He's missing!"

"What difference does it make?" the sergeant repeated. "She wants to know what difference it makes!" He looked at Hermux and shrugged helplessly.

"Well?" Linka asked.

"It makes a whole world of difference," the sergeant lectured. "If it's county, I fill out a county form for the sheriff. In triplicate." He held up a pink form to prove his point. "But if it's city, it goes to the police. That's a blue form like this. And that's in duplicate. Totally different. So, which is it?"

"How do we know?" asked Hermux.

"Where is he?"

"We don't know. That's why we're here!"

"Where he'd disappear from?"

"We don't know that either."

The sergeant capped his pen. "Then there's not much I can do."

"We've got a good description," said Hermux.

"I guess that's better than nothing," the sergeant said. Reluctantly he uncapped his pen again. "Shoot!"

Hermux started over. "He's male, squirrel, mid-to-late thirties, last seen wearing a brown tweed overcoat. It's missing some buttons, and the elbows are worn through. And a knitted cap. Navy blue."

The sergeant capped his pen and closed his notebook.

"You're in luck," he said and smiled, not too unpleasantly either. "He left town. The day before yesterday."

"What do you mean, he left town?" asked Linka.

"Just what I said," the sergeant answered. He opened his notebook and flipped back through the pages. "Thursday. Seven A.M. Anonymous caller reports suspicious vagrant loitering at bus station. Male, squirrel, mid-to-late thirties, tweed overcoat, blue cap. Appears disoriented. Possibly dangerous. Officer dispatched to scene. Suspect interviewed. Claims family emergency. Needs money for bus ticket. Officer authorizes ticket purchase from Mayor's Good Samaritan Fund. Suspect escorted to bus and cautioned not to return to Thorny End. Bus departs at 7:30 nonstop to Pinchester."

Linka and Hermux were both relieved for Plank's sake and for Twigg's, but they were a little disappointed in Plank nonetheless. She and Hermux conferred privately. "That certainly wasn't very fatherly of him. Now what do we do?"

"There's still the dead body," said Hermux. He looked up at the sergeant. "We want to report a dead body."

"Oh, sure!" the sergeant said. "A dead body. I can't wait to hear. I suppose you don't know where this one is either." The desk phone rang then. "If it's quite all right with you, though, I'll just take this itsy-bitsy little call before we get started." He swiveled away from them and answered the phone.

"Sheriff's office! City police! Sergeant Wishrigg speaking!" He listened and began to scribble in his notebook. Moments later, he slammed down the receiver and stood up. "Sorry!

202

We've got an emergency on our hands! You'll have to come back later." Then he donned his cap and raced from the room, leaving Hermux and Linka alone. From outside came the sounds of sirens.

"What do you think it is?" asked Linka.

Hermux stood on tiptoe and reached across the desk for the sergeant's notebook. He turned it to face him. He could barely read the careless scrawl.

Saturday, 10:03 A.M. Caller reports emergency at Reezor Bleesom estate. Dead roses. Sending all available officers!

He showed it to Linka. "I told you it was dangerous to invite her to a party."

"Let's get back to the island," she said, "before Twigg and Terfle get restless."

Chapter 52
RISE AND SHINE!

Reezor had spent the night before his party attending to the last-minute details that would make it the social event of the season. He inspected every inch of his estate, beginning with the rose garden. Of all the things he had accomplished in his life, he was most proud of his garden. Designing it like an enormous rose was a stroke of brilliance, he thought. At the garden's center was a plaza with a fountain. Reezor toured the garden in his customized golf cart. One hundred acres of *Rosa fragrantissimas*, and this was their moment of perfection. The sight was dazzling. The scent intoxicating. By any standard the garden was a smashing success—even more wonderful than Reezor had hoped. And tomorrow everyone he knew would be there to share it with him!

When Reezor had bought the land and announced his intentions to build his dream house, his friends had laughed at him. He was crazy to build a house so far from Pinchester—the center of every*thing* that mattered to every*one* who mattered. But that is exactly what drove him to do it. He needed a place to get away from it all. A place to think. Besides, like Tucka, who had trained him, Reezor was a control freak. He wanted to control every aspect of his perfumes from the flower to the bottle. That was why he'd planted his own roses.

Back at the house Reezor continued his inspection, starting with the gift bags that each guest would receive as they arrived at the party. Working for Tucka had taught him the importance of gift bags. Each bag contained a signed color photo of him; a glossy illustrated booklet that told the story of his life, beginning with his very earliest memories; a souvenir key chain with his initials in rhinestones; and a sample spray bottle of Time to Smell the Roses. He examined Primm's bouquets that filled the house and spilled out onto the terrace. Finally he gazed out over the pool of water lilies. Above the dark water floated Thirxen Ghoulter's dragonflies, delicate and still. The effect was enchanting.

The party was scheduled for morning because that was the best time to smell roses. Reezor wouldn't appear until all the guests had arrived. Once they were gathered on the garden plaza, he would make his entrance on his parade float. He had mentally rehearsed it all week, and he could hardly wait.

At bedtime he left a note for his staff. He was not to be disturbed *for any reason whatsoever* before 10:00 A.M. the next morning. He wanted to be fresh for the celebration. Then he turned out the lights and retired to the master suite. He put on his sleeping mask, crawled into bed, and fell asleep.

Reezor had bought his bed at a castle liquidation sale, and it had once belonged to a real king. The posters that supported the canopy were carved with garlands of roses, and the canopy was topped by a huge royal crown. It had been love at first sight. Reezor had instructed Primm to use the bed as the model for his parade float.

The next morning Reezor slept late. He took a long, lazy

bath and dressed with care. Refreshed and eager, he appeared in the kitchen at precisely 9:58. A double skinny no-whip extra-hot butterscotch-caramel latte waited for him on the counter as always. He drank it down with pleasure. Then he took the elevator to the garage, where his parade float proudly awaited.

Primm had reproduced Reezor's bed down to the last detail of the crown. But on a much bigger scale. And she'd covered it entirely with roses.

"It's a work of art!" exclaimed Reezor.

"There's been a problem," Reezor's assistant began to explain.

Reezor raised his paw imperiously. "Not one more word! I am in a wonderful mood today. I do not want to hear anything negative until this party is over! Does everyone understand that? Now, help me up there and start the engines! It's time to party!"

Reezor climbed up into the bed. He tucked himself in beneath the thick rose comforter and settled his head on the oversized rose pillow. He closed his eyes and pretended to be asleep. He kept them closed all the way to the fountain.

As they neared the plaza, he could feel the crowd's excitement. This was a day they would all remember for years to come!

Finally, when he could stand it no more, he threw back the comforter and sat up in bed. He pretended to yawn and sniffed the air hungrily.

He opened his eyes and shouted, "It must be time to smell the roses!" He looked around, expecting to see a horde of happy, smiling faces.

But there was only one smile—Tucka's.

"Reezor," she cooed at him. "I just want you to know that no matter what else happens, you can always count on me!" She gestured beyond the plaza. "It's simply tragic! Nothing else can quite describe it."

The last thing Reezor recalled thinking that morning was that Tucka's lips looked remarkably plump and firm. Then he looked out at his roses and saw that all one hundred acres of them had been reduced to black and withered stumps.

Chapter 53
TO BE OR NOT TO BE

Twigg watched the spider advance. His finger twitched, but he held his fire. "Not yet," he told himself. "Not yet." He had faced bullies before, and they all had a weak spot. The trick was to find it in time. The candle was sputtering now. At any moment it might go out.

The spider was barely eight feet away from him when it paused. Fangs extended and ready to strike, it reared up slightly on its legs to gauge the distance for its final attack. And as it did, its left eye caught the light.

Twigg aimed at the eye. As he released the stone, the candle guttered and died, plunging the tunnel into darkness.

A long moment of silence followed. Then something soft and heavy crumpled onto the floor.

"Terfle?" Twigg called. He fumbled in his pocket for matches. He found the candle stub on the floor and relit it.

"Terfle?" he repeated hopefully. "Are you there?"

She was. Terfle emerged from the shadows, circled Twigg, and settled on his head like a ruby returning to its crown.

Twigg hurried through the door and closed it firmly behind

them. Beyond the door the tunnel broadened and then split again. At the intersection hung a handpainted sign.

← *To the meadow*
To the barn →

This tunnel was built and is maintained by the moles of the Jeckel Island Commune.

Please treat it with respect.
Peace!

The decision didn't take long. After their time in the tunnels, they were both ready for sunlight and fresh air. The left branch of the tunnel ended in a flight of steps. The steps led up to a trapdoor, but the door would not open. Twigg set Terfle and the candle down. Then he braced his shoulder against the door and pushed up with all his strength. Twigg was not yet full grown, but he was strong nonetheless. The door gave slightly. He heaved again, and the door sprang open, taking Twigg with it. He landed on his tail in a bed of gravel. Terfle followed close behind.

As their eyes adjusted to the light, they realized that they were not outside in a meadow after all. They were inside a large greenhouse. The greenhouse was filled with roses and the roses were covered with bees. The bees noticed them as well. A few scouts approached. One flew very close to Twigg's head. He couldn't resist the impulse to wave it away. The scout returned; this time it landed on Twigg's ear and stung him.

"Yeow!" Twigg leapt to his feet, launching Terfle high into the air. "Let's get out of here!"

There was one door in the greenhouse. As Twigg discovered, it was locked.

"Help!" he shouted, and pounded on the glass. Through the glass he could see a beekeeper's costume, complete with thick gloves and a heavy veil, hanging from a hook on the wall. He kicked at the glass, but the glass did not so much as crack. Terfle flew past him and pointed behind her.

Twigg turned in time to see a swarm of bees organize itself into fight formation. Row after row of bees waiting for some signal to attack. Twigg was frozen on the spot, unable to move in any direction.

It was Terfle who acted. She chose a spot at the center of the bees' formation and flew directly at it. The bees drew back. They had lived sheltered lives in the greenhouse, and none of them knew from experience how dangerous this unexpected creature might be. They watched as Terfle sped past them, banked, and then headed straight for their hive. Then they followed in hot pursuit.

Twigg watched helplessly as the bees overtook Terfle. They forced her to a landing on the ramp of the hive, then they surrounded her. They took her prisoner and marched her toward the hive's entrance. They would let the queen decide her fate. At the threshold Terfle stopped and turned back to wave good-bye to Twigg.

Terfle was proud of herself. Maybe she was only a ladybug after all. And he was only a squirrel. But she'd bought him a few moments of precious time. If only he would use them.

"Terfle! Come back!" Twigg yelled.

Then the guards pushed her roughly inside.

He started after her, but the bees turned their attention back to him. Twigg knew he was no match for a hive full of angry bees. The trapdoor was his only chance.

Chapter 54
EMPTY NESTERS

Hermux and Linka had worked out the details of the plan as they rowed across the bay. It seemed like a good plan.

They would fetch Twigg and Terfle and then get off the island as quickly as possible. Then they would all fly back to Pinchester, where they would get right to work picking up Plank's trail while it was still fresh.

Plank had a two-day head start, but there were several promising avenues to pursue.

First, Plank might have friends or acquaintances in the city, and Twigg might know who they are. They would each be contacted and questioned.

Then they would interview the employees at the bus station and canvas the neighborhood for people who might have seen Plank arrive.

And they would put up a poster and offer a reward for information leading to the discovery of Plank's whereabouts. Working with Twigg, Terfle could draw a portrait of Plank. They would use that to print a poster that they would put up all over town.

It would only be a matter of time.

Once Plank was found, they would delicately broach the

subject of the DeRosenquill family ties. And he and Twigg could decide what to do from there.

"Once they're settled, we can come back and investigate the rest," Hermux said. "We could stay at the inn. It might make a nice honeymoon."

"Just what I've always dreamed of," sighed Linka. "A missing corpse. Killer bees. And Tucka Mertslin. What could be more romantic?"

They landed the rowboat on the far side of the island and hid it just like Twigg had shown them. Things were looking up. They were in high spirits as they hiked back to the tree house.

"We're back!" Hermux announced as he clambered up through the hole in the floor. "And we brought donuts!"

But the tree house was empty.

He called down to Linka, "There's nobody here!"

Chapter 55
BAD NEWS TRAVELS FAST

Tucka was having too much fun to drive back to Pinchester after Reezor's party as she had planned. Besides, she felt like celebrating. She was so delighted with the results of Killum's rose defoliation spray that she thought he deserved a surprise party. She changed back into her disguise, shopped for the party, and called the island to order the ferry to pick her up.

At five o'clock she called Clareen from her cabin. The evening newspapers would be out by now, and she was dying to hear Moozella's account of Reezor's party.

"What do you have for me?" she asked. "Start with Moozella."

"I thought you'd like it," Clareen said. "I bought six copies."

"Read!" Tucka told her.

Clareen cleared her voice and began.

WRECK & RUIN
AT REEZOR'S
RESORT RETREAT

Guests Gape As Glamour Guru Goes GaGa

A Moozella Corkin Exclusive

THORNY END, June 8—It was the party of the season. And we all know that no one throws a party like **Nature Boy Reezor Bleesom.** Now we know that no one throws a fit like him either. (Don't worry, I'll have photos for you tomorrow!) Luckily doctors were on hand to sedate him when disaster struck this morning, mysteriously destroying one hundred acres of premium roses at his luxury bachelor pad in the Paddlepick Valley.

Pinchester socialites and VIPs who were on hand for the celebration-turned-meltdown were quick to express their support. Fellow mogul and beauty industry spokeswoman **Tucka Mertslin,** sporting a pair of newly Luscious Lips, called an impromptu press conference to announce the formation of the **Emergency Committee to Save the Roses.** "I've alerted my team of scientists, and they're already working on it," she said. "It's bad enough to think that Reezor may be completely wiped out. I want to reassure the public that no matter what it takes, it won't happen to anyone else."

Androse DeRosenquill was also at the scene, and he knows a thing or two about roses. He spoke to me after surveying the damage. "If I didn't know better, I'd think the fields had been poisoned. But only a sociopath would do something like that. I think the culprit must be a deadly, fast-acting parasite like *Fungus speedis lethalis*. It's extremely rare here. But the *fragrantissima* is very sensitive to it."

Tucka Mertslin's Luscious Lip-Fix
will be available soon at
Orsik & Arrbale.

"Excellent!" said Tucka.
"There's more," said Clareen.
"Read it!"
Clareen read on.

Sympathy cards can be sent to
Reezor Bleesom c/o
Dusty Oaks Sanatorium,
Paddlepick Valley.

Tucka tittered. "Poor dear! I hope they gave him a padded cell. I'm sure he'd be more comfortable with plenty of padding."

"There's still more," said Clareen.

"Do tell!" Tucka smiled and waved at herself in the mirror. She couldn't remember when she had had this much fun.

Clareen continued to read. "See related story on page two." She paused.

"Well?" Tucka asked. "Read it!"

"You're sure?"

"I'm sure! This is just getting good!"

"All right," Clareen said.

RUMOR SPARKS RUSH AT LOCAL DEPARTMENT STORE—
Perfume Counter Under Siege

Hundreds of anxious shoppers descended on Orsik & Arrbale this afternoon as an outbreak of deadly fungus at the Reezor Bleesom rose gardens in Thorny End fueled reports of a possible shortage of the company's best-selling perfume, Time to Smell the Roses.

Store president Enrinky Doofmuller said, "I've never seen anything like it. It was pure panic. We sold every bottle in the store in

> fifteen minutes. And we've doubled our next order."
>
> A spokeswoman at Reezor Bleesom Fragrances assured reporters that the designer's trademark perfume would continue despite recent glitches. "If anything," she said, "we'll be increasing production." Late this afternoon the company announced an emergency agreement with DeRosenquill & Son guaranteeing continued supplies of rose oil for the foreseeable future.

Clareen paused again.

"Are you absolutely finished now?" Tucka asked. Her smile was long gone, replaced by a genuine and very impressive pout. "Because if you are, I have other things to do." She didn't wait for Clareen's response. She hung up the phone.

"DeRosenquill to the rescue," she muttered to herself. "It's always DeRosenquill. Well, we'll just see about that."

She dialed Killium's extension in the laboratory.

"Dr. Wollar speaking. May I help you?"

"I certainly hope so," said Tucka. "How are you fixed for *Fungus speedis lethalis*?"

Chapter 56
TALE SPIN

Twigg crawled up through the hole and collapsed on the floor of the tree house. Hermux and Linka watched him with alarm. He was covered with dirt and strands of spiderweb clung to the fur of his tail.

Linka knelt at his side. She felt his forehead. "Are you okay?"

Twigg glanced up at her and began to cry.

"Where's Terfle?" said Hermux. He held the empty Sport-a-Pet in his hand.

Twigg buried his face in his arms. He was trembling all over.

Linka spoke to him very gently. "It's all right, Twigg. Just tell us what happened."

"It's all my fault," he said miserably. "I don't think Terfle wanted to go. We should have stayed here like you said."

"Where did you go?" Hermux asked.

"The tunnel."

Hermux winced. "And what happened?"

Twigg began to speak in a rush, reliving the story as he told it, recalling details of the candle, the stick, and the darkness,

Terfle's nerves, the feeling of adventure, their excitement at finding the door in the tunnel. "And then suddenly the spider was right behind us! I didn't know what to do! I panicked. I ran throught the door and Terfle fell off."

Hermux didn't want to hear any more. He wanted to cover his ears and close his eyes.

"And the first shot killed it," said Twigg. He couldn't help feeling a moment of pride, however short-lived.

"The spider?" Hermux asked. "It's dead?"

Twigg nodded.

Hermux hardly dared to hope. "And what about Terfle?"

"She was okay," said Twigg.

"Okay?" Hermux danced for joy. "Okay!" he sang. "Did you hear that, Linka? She's okay! Why didn't you say so? Where is she now?"

It was not an easy thing to say. But Twigg had to say it.

"She's not here. She was captured by the bees."

Chapter 57
POSITIVE THINK TANK

"Be careful!" Killium warned her. "It's extremely concentrated. One drop and the lab would be contaminated forever."

Tucka held the vial up to the light. Inside was a perfectly clear, perfectly harmless-looking liquid. She read the label fondly. *"Fungus speedis lethalis.* It even sounds nice. Do I want to know how you got it?"

"No. You don't," said Killium. He took the vial from her. "What I need now is the right container. We've got to get it into the air, but we can't use the sprayers again. They're too big and too obvious. People will be watching for anything suspicious."

Tucka looked around the lab. Her eyes lighted on the gift bag from Reezor's party. "I've got an idea," she said. She opened the bag and rifled through it. "What about this?" She held up the purse-sized sample of Time to Smell the Roses.

"You are wicked!" said Killium.

"Look who's talking!" she responded. She waggled her whiskers flirtatiously. "While you do that, I think I'll freshen up. If we're going to pay a visit to the DeRosenquills this evening, I'd better look my best."

An hour later she was back. Tucka had dressed for evening

in a tight, beaded, jet-black coatdress that showed plenty of cleavage. Her fur was swept up into a beehive with the black widow perched firmly on top like a pillbox hat. Her lips were a vicious red.

"Do you think it's too formal for Thorny End?" she asked.

Killium studied her. "Nonsense," he said. "You look like the girl next door!" Killium was standing in front of the rolling whiteboard. He was studying a crudely drawn map of the Villa DeRosenquill.

Tucka answered with a coquettish air kiss before turning to the map. "What's this?"

"Our target. I had Skuhl draw it for me. But we'll need someone to show us exactly where the *fragrantissimas* are planted if you really want this to work."

"Oh, we don't need to worry about that," Tucka said demurely. "I think Androse DeRosenquill will be happy to show us around. He's got an eye for beautiful women. And he's not half bad for a squirrel his age."

Killium felt a dull ache in his ribs. He wondered if this was jealousy. Then he remembered that he'd pulled something hauling the crate through the garden. His thoughts were interrupted by an enormous sigh of pleasure from Tucka.

"You know, Killium," she began. "I'm having such fun. I got to thinking while I was getting dressed. There's no reason we have to stop with Reezor."

"What do you mean?"

"We could move on to other things. Other smells! Don't you see?" Tucka was in one of her visionary moods. She began to pace back and forth in front of the whiteboard. "Reezor's loss is our gain. With him out of business, the market will be wide open for a new rose perfume. I was thinking of calling it A Rose

Is a Rose Is a Rose. Only it won't be. It'll be artificial. It's only a fraction of the cost. It's a perfect business model. We choose a natural scent. We duplicate it artificially, and we patent it. Then we destroy the natural source. And we own a monopoly!"

"A smell monopoly! I think I get it!"

"I thought you would," Tucka said. She flipped the whiteboard over and wrote:

Goal: global domination

"What about gardenias?" asked Killium.

"Good! They're popular. And they're very fragile! Gardenias are an excellent choice!" Tucka wrote *gardenias* on the whiteboard.

"How about jasmine? Everyone loves jasmine!"

Tucka added *jasmine* to the list. Then, she said, "Lilies!"

"Lilies!" shouted Killium. "Perfect! And sweet peas!"

"Good! Good!" Tucka crowed. "But we've got to think even bigger! Thinking positive is thinking BIG. We've got to think outside the box!"

Tucka closed her eyes and visualized what global domination would look like. It was lovely. Then she had a thought. "Fresh-baked chocolate chip cookies!"

"Wow!" Killium commented. "Way outside the box!"

"But could it be done?" Tucka asked.

Killium pondered.

"Difficult," he concluded. "But doable."

Tucka added *chocolate chip cookies* to the board.

"What about coffee?" Killium asked.

"Coffee!" sang Tucka.

"Toast!"

Toast! wrote Tucka.

"Popcorn!" whooped Killium.

"Popcorn!" echoed Tucka.

Tucka's pacing slowed to a stop. Her vicious red lips were pursed in thought. Then she squealed. "I've got it! The ultra-concept of all time!"

"Say it!" Killium commanded.

"Babies!" Tucka gasped. "Babies! Mothers would pay anything on earth for the smell of babies. If we can make scent-free babies and then supply the scent, we'll be richer than Ortolina Perriflot!"

Gloating was one of Tucka's favorite pasttimes. But there was no time for it now. Someone was knocking on the door. Tucka concealed herself behind the whiteboard while Killium went to answer it. He returned carrying a stack of boxes.

"Delivery," he said. "For you."

"Oh! What perfect timing!" said Tucka. "Put them on the table. I almost forgot!"

Chapter 58
HANG~UPS

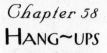

Hermux peeked through the trapdoor.

"I think I see it," he said. "That looks like a beehive there against the far wall."

"That's it," said Twigg. "That's where they took her."

"May I look?" asked Linka.

"Be careful," said Hermux. "Don't let them spot you."

Hermux pointed out the hive to Linka.

"And where's the door?" she asked.

Twigg showed her. "But's it locked," he said. "And I couldn't break the glass. Besides the trapdoor, it's the only way out."

"The important thing is to stay very calm," Linka informed them. "Bees can sense it if you're frightened or angry. That's what stirs them up. Maybe if we move very slowly—" She broke off without finishing. Bees swarmed from the hive at an alarming rate and rocketed straight for the trapdoor. She shoved Hermux back, ducked down and let the trapdoor drop shut.

"I thought you said to stay calm," said Hermux.

A sharp rat-a-tat-tat struck the door.

"We'll try that later!" said Linka. "Right now, let's move!"

They retreated back into the tunnel.

"Now what do we do?" asked Hermux.

Twigg remembered something. "I saw a beekeeping suit. In the other room up there. Maybe we can get to it through the barn."

He was right. Following the other branch of the tunnel, they found another set of steps. And another trapdoor. Cautiously Hermux pushed it open and poked his head out. The trapdoor opened into a storeroom. It was attached to the greenhouse. Hermux could hear music and laughter coming from somewhere nearby. Someone was having a party.

He climbed out and motioned for Linka and Twigg to join him, putting a finger to his lips to warn them to be quiet.

The beekeeper's suit hung on the wall just as Twigg had said. It was heavy-duty canvas with a hard helmet and a wire veil. Hermux wasted no time. He put on the helmet and lowered the veil while Linka took down the canvas suit. Behind it hung a ragged overcoat.

"That's Dad's coat!" Twigg cried. "If he's supposed to be in Pinchester, what's it doing here?"

Next door, the party sounds came to a sudden stop.

Chapter 59
PARTY CRASHERS

The door flew open, and Tucka stood there with a large butcher knife in one hand.

"We're having a little surprise party," she said. "I don't remember inviting any guests, but why don't you join us?" She motioned them forward with the knife.

Twigg was closest to the door. He went first. As he slouched past her, Tucka's practiced eye took in his defiant attitude, his unkempt fur, and his dirty clothes and boots.

"If the modeling agency sent you all the way down here," she said acidly, "you're too late. We cast the Wild Rumpus ad last week."

Linka stepped by with her head averted from the light.

"Don't be shy, dear," Tucka admonished. "We're all friends here."

Hermux appeared in the doorway, his face hidden by the beekeeper's veil.

"And who is this?" Tucka inquired. "A mystery guest? I live for mystery!" Using the point of the butcher knife, she slowly lifted the veil until Hermux peeked out at her.

"Surprise!" he said.

"Tantamoq!" she gasped. The black widow wobbled precariously on her head. Tucka flipped the helmet from his head and rested the blade delicately against his throat. "I should have known! For ten cents I'd slit your throat. But I suppose that would be murder, wouldn't it?" She smiled spitefully and withdrew the knife. She pointed it at Linka. "And this must be the irrepressible Ms. Perflinger! Whatever brings you two to Jeckel Island? Do tell! Snooping as usual?"

Hermux thought that honesty was the best policy. "I was hired to find a missing person—"

"I'm sure that's all very fascinating," Tucka said. "As you can see, none of us are missing. But since you're here, you may as well have some cake." She left Hermux standing and crossed the lab to Killium's desk, where a large birthday cake frosted with thick red roses sat waiting. As she passed the whiteboard, she deftly picked up an eraser and wiped it clean.

"Killium, don't just stand there! Give our unexpected guests some napkins while I cut. I'm afraid you'll have to use your fingers. We're short on forks."

Killium still hadn't recovered from the shock of Hermux and friends' sudden appearance.

"Oh, dear!" Tucka apologized. "I'm sorry. I haven't introduced everyone. Killium? This is Hermux Tantamoq, my neighbor. We're terribly close. Mr. Tantamoq is a watchmaker. And a professional pain in the neck. This is his little friend Ms. Perflinger. She's a pilot. Or so she says. And this is—" She pointed at Twigg. "Let me guess—Hermux's new assistant!"

"My name is Twigg," he said proudly. "I like your hat."

"Thank you, Twigg. It was a gift from someone very special.

I hope you realize you're working for an idiot!" Then she handed him a piece of cake.

When Tucka offered Hermux a piece, he was tempted, on principle, to refuse. But it was late afternoon, and he had missed lunch again. He licked the frosting cautiously, then took a bite.

"And who are you?" Linka asked Killium. "You haven't said."

"I'm Doctor Wollar. Killium Wollar."

"And I suppose you're the director of Tucka's secret lab here." It was only a guess on Linka's part, but from the look on Tucka's face, it was a good one. "Mmmm, Tucka, my compliments. This is very good cake."

"I'm glad you think so," said Tucka. "Now it's time to open presents!"

"Oh, boy!" said Killium.

"Start with that one," she directed.

It was a big box sealed with black satin ribbon. Killium ripped through the ribbon. He tore off the lid and pulled out a mountain of tissue paper. Then he stopped and stared down into the box.

"I hope you like it!" said Tucka. "I thought it would be perfect for occasions just like this."

"Thank you!" he stammered. "It's . . . It's . . ."

"Perfect?" Tucka suggested.

"That it!" agreed Killium. "It's perfect. I've always wanted one!"

Tucka beamed with pleasure. "I thought so."

This was Twigg's very first birthday party. And with all the excitement of cake and candles and presents, he could stand the suspense no longer. "What is it?" he asked.

Killium lifted his gift from the box.

"It's an automatic pistol," he said. "Isn't that swell?"

Tucka winked at Killium and nodded toward Hermux, Linka, and Twigg. "Show our guests how it works!"

"Put your hands up!" he told them. "And keep your mouths shut."

Like any good surprise, they hadn't seen it coming.

"I've always wanted to say that!" Killium said.

"And you said it very well," Tucka assured him.

Twigg was slow to raise his hands. At first he thought the gun must be some sort of party game. Maybe it was a game that adults liked. Or maybe it was a game peculiar to mice. Hermux and Linka seemed to know the rules. They wasted no time putting their hands straight up in the air. Hermux even dropped his cake. But Twigg didn't feel like playing games just then. And frankly he was surprised that Hermux and Linka did. At that very moment Terfle was in danger. "And what about my dad?" he thought.

"Get your hands up, boy!" Killium growled. He waved the gun for emphasis. "Before I plug you!"

Hermux took a step toward Killium, and Killium leveled the gun at Hermux.

"You want to be first?" he asked.

Hermux froze. And at that moment Twigg understood that this was real. And these strange people were not nice mice. His temper flared. "How did you get my dad's coat and hat?"

"Your dad?" Killium stammered.

"It's hanging right in there. We found it behind the beekeeper's suit!" Twigg was really mad now. "Where is he?"

Killium opened his mouth to speak but nothing came out. He looked as though he had seen a ghost. Or maybe the son of a ghost.

"Do you know this boy?" Tucka asked.

"No," Killium managed. This party was turning out to have too many surprises for him.

"Then how do you know his father?" Tucka demanded.

"I didn't know him!"

"Didn't?" Tucka sensed something amiss. One look at Hermux's face confirmed it. "Tantamoq? What's going on?"

"Why don't you ask him?" Hermux said, and pointed to Killium. "While you're at it, ask him about the body in the rose garden. Who's that?"

"Body?" Tucka asked, her voice rising abruptly. "In whose garden?"

"Yours!" said Linka. "I traced the ownership of the island."

"Killium!" Tucka commanded. "You'd better explain. And it had better be good!"

In a life that had been devoted primarily to pranks, Killium had been caught more often than he cared to admit. He had usually managed to escape with little or no punishment by thinking fast and talking even faster. In this case his lips began moving long before his mind started to work.

"Okay! Okay!" he said petulantly. "I bought the coat and the hat from a bum. I thought it would be a good Hallowe'en costume."

"How quaint!" said Tucka. "Was he a peddler?"

"My dad was not a bum!" Twigg said. "And he wasn't a peddler. You stole that coat!"

"I did not!" Killium's mind was beginning to hatch a story.

"He showed up here looking for work. I felt sorry for him and I hired him for a day. To tend the bees. I keep a hive for the honey."

"We know all about the bees!" said Hermux.

"What could you possibly know?" taunted Tucka.

"We know they're killers!" Hermux shot back.

"It's a mere figure of speech," said Tucka disdainfully. "An affectionate name I gave them."

"No," said Linka. "It's the truth. The bees have already killed one person. They could kill others."

"Killium?" Tucka said. The words MASSIVE LAWSUIT rang in her head like the bell of doom.

"They're lying!"

"Then what about the body in the garden?" asked Hermux.

"I don't know anything about a body," Killium vowed.

"Liar!" said Linka. "We watched you bury it last night!"

"Where's my father?" Twigg demanded.

"He wanted to get away from you, you little brat!" Killium snarled. "He was trying to earn the money to buy a bus ticket to Pinchester! Ask the police!"

"We did ask the police," Hermux said evenly. "The odd thing is that you've got his coat right here, and yet he was seen wearing that coat when he got on the bus."

Killium hadn't considered that. But before he could come up with an answer, Twigg charged.

"You killed my father!" he screamed.

Killium was slow to react. Tucka, who had been in a number of ticklish situations before, was not. She stuck her foot out and tripped Twigg. He fell flat on his face. She put a high-heeled foot on his back and pinned him to the floor.

"Hold still!" she told him.

"You're in deep doo-doo," Hermux said.

For once, she agreed with him. "Killium, you've got exactly one minute to tell me what's going on here. And I want the truth!"

"All right," he said. "This squirrel showed up looking for work. And the bees were getting so aggressive that they were starting to make me nervous. I didn't like going in there anymore. He told me he wasn't afraid of bees. So I hired him."

"And he's dead?" Tucka asked.

"It was an accident. How was I to know the bees would kill him?"

Twigg howled in rage, "You murderer! Let me up! Let me —"

"Stop it!" Tucka warned. A well-placed jab of her heel and Twigg went limp.

"Did you at least warn him they were dangerous?" asked Hermux.

"Did he have a safety suit?" asked Linka. "That one in there is too small for a squirrel!"

Killium only shrugged.

"Who else knows about this?" Tucka asked Hermux and Linka.

"We've informed a number of people," Hermux said. "All the proper authorities."

"Now who's lying?" Tucka pursed her luscious lips and considered her predicament. "You've gotten me into a real mess, Killium." She remembered the decision-making techniques she had learned years ago, right there at the institute, in fact. And she made an executive decision. "You'll have to kill them all," she told Killium, as though it were the most obvious thing in the world.

234

"Kill them?"

"That's right. Otherwise they'll talk. And it will cost me a fortune."

"Why me?" Killium moaned.

"You got us into this. You get us out! If you hurry, we can dump their bodies in the bay on the way to dinner and still get there in time for our reservation."

"He already tried that once," Linka said. "It didn't work. Did it, Killium?"

"Start with Tantamoq!" Tucka said. "I've waited for this for a long time."

Reluctantly Killium aimed the gun at Hermux and prepared to fire. But pulling the trigger was harder than he imagined.

"Wait!" he said, brightening up. "I've got a better idea."

Chapter 61
BEE STILL MY HEART!

"I would say that it's been nice knowing you, Tantamoq, but we both know it hasn't." With that Tucka gave him a final kick in the bottom and sent him sprawling into the greenhouse after Linka and Twigg. Killium slammed the door and slid all three bolts into place. "Don't worry," Tucka consoled them through the reinforced glass. "You'll hardly feel a thing. Maybe a slight pinprick at first. And then you'll become very sleepy and drift away."

"That's a lie, and you know it!" said Hermux.

"Well, at least you'll have beautiful lips!" Tucka countered cheerily. "Look at mine!" She pressed her lips against the glass, producing a grotesque kissy smear.

"You're disgusting!" Linka said, shaking a helpless fist at her.

"Oh, lighten up, Linka! We can't all be perfect little misses like you!" Tucka turned to Killium. "I think we've wasted enough of our time here. Where are the bees, anyway? Shouldn't they be here by now?"

Killium smacked the glass with his hand. On the other side of the greenhouse the first scouts left the hive and took to the air. They proceeded to do a flyover to assess the new intruders. Twigg hit the ground. Hermux rushed to the door and pounded on it.

"Completely unbreakable!" Killium told him. "Five-year guarantee. You couldn't get through it with a sledgehammer!"

Hermux moved to a window and continued to pound.

"Let us out or you'll be sorry!" he vowed.

Instead of answering, Tucka directed his attention to the hive, where a seemingly endless swarm of bees poured from the entrance. Then she turned away, taking Killium's arm and waltzing toward the door. "I don't think we need to see this, do we? I don't want to spoil my appetite. And besides, after dinner, we have some important business to attend to. Don't we?"

Chapter 62
ROYAL RECEPTION

A storm cloud of bees spilled out of the hive. They assembled in three arrow-shaped squadrons pointing right at Hermux, Linka, and Twigg.

Hermux began to edge toward the trapdoor entrance in the center of the greenhouse. As he moved, one of the squadrons moved with him.

"I'll try to get the door open," Hermux said in a calm and even voice. "If I do, I'll try to draw them away while you two get out. Then I'll follow." Under his breath he added, "If I can."

Hermux reached the trapdoor and tried gently to lift it. But the door would not yield to gentle pressure. It would be necessary to give it a good heave. Hermux sensed that the sudden movement would trigger the bees' attack. He met Linka's eyes for what he thought might possibly be the last time.

"We'll be out of here in no time!" he whispered.

"Of course we will!" she whispered back.

He could see tears in her eyes. "And we'll have a beautiful wedding!"

"Yes, we will!"

"In a country inn, just like you wanted. Twigg, you're invited too!"

"Thanks, Hermux," he said bravely.

"I'm really sorry about your father, Twigg. I'm sorry you had to find out like that." Hermux's voice quavered. It was then or never for the trapdoor. He braced his knees to pull, but before he could move, the bees moved first. The entire squadron rushed him from behind and knocked him over. He landed squarely on top of the trapdoor. He braced himself for the first sting.

But it didn't come.

Then the bees returned, flying so close to him that he could feel the brush of their wings against the tips of his ears. But still no sting. He sat up.

"What are they waiting for?" he asked.

"I don't know," answered Linka.

"Something's happening at the hive," Twigg said. "Look!"

The bees had withdrawn to the side of the greenhouse and hovered now on either side of the hive.

"It's looks like they're waiting for someone," said Linka.

"I hope it's not a bigger bee," said Hermux. He scrambled to the edge of the trapdoor and struggled again to get it open.

"I'm afraid it is!" said Linka. "It's enormous!"

As much as he did not want to look, he could not resist. Two lines of bees stood at attention as the colossal golden body emerged. A furious buzz from the airborne troops greeted it.

"Oh, no!" Hermux moaned as the behemoth bee extended its amber wings. "We're goners!"

A throne appeared, carried by attendants, which the over-sized bee mounted clumsily.

"That must be the queen!" said Twigg.

"Do you think they're going to use us for entertainment?" Hermux wondered out loud. By now he had managed to hook his fingers under the edge of the door, and he was pulling in earnest. He thought he was starting to make some progress.

There was a flurry of activity at the hive's entrance. Then four bees marched from the interior, apparently escorting someone of some importance. They bowed before the queen and withdrew, leaving their charge behind. It was a familiar-looking figure, compact, round, and glossy red.

"Terfle!" shouted Hermux.

Terfle curtsied long and low before the queen. Then she turned, opened her shell, and flew to her friends.

Chapter 63
COURTESY CALL

Tucka liked everything about the Villa DeRosenquill. She liked the stone gates. She liked the broad drive that swept up to the house through the rose gardens. She liked the brick steps and the terrace. She liked the grand entrance with its carved oak doors. She even liked Tarp, the surly butler. Everything she saw said OLD MONEY in capital letters. Tucka loved money. She had plenty of it herself. But she adored OLD money. And that was obviously the kind of money that the DeRosenquills had.

"Good evening," Tucka greeted Tarp in a tone that that was intended to be every bit as condescending as he was surly. "I'm here on behalf of the Emergency Committee to Save the Roses."

"Never heard of it," said Tarp. He was hard to impress.

"You will, I assure you," said Tucka. "I am Tucka Mertslin, and this is my associate, Mr. uh—Clovlinnik. Please tell Mr. DeRosenquill that we're here to see him on urgent committee business. The future of roses is at stake."

"Right," said Tarp, still unimpressed. "Wait here."

He went to find Androse, leaving Tucka and Killium alone

in the entrance hall. She headed straight for the living room and moved around it quickly, examining the rugs, the furniture, and the family portraits. She appraised each piece quickly at current market value and kept a running total in her head. When she finished her circuit of the room, she was thoroughly dazzled by the figure.

The thought occurred to her that if her plans went according to plan, the DeRosenquills could soon find themselves out of business too. They might consider a reasonable offer to take the Villa DeRosenquill off their impoverished hands.

While Tucka was lost in house and garden fantasies, Killium had other things on his mind. Up until that evening, with the exception of a few pointless pranks, he had led a pretty innocent life. Of course, there was the death of the homeless squirrel and stealing his body and all that. But really, even the toughest jury would have to admit that that had been an accident, although he should have known better about letting the poor fool go into the greenhouse without a beekeeper's suit. But forcing the Tantamoq fellow and his girlfriend and the squirrel boy into the greenhouse and locking them in had been another thing entirely. It had seemed like fun at the time. But in hindsight, he wasn't so sure. It sounded suspiciously like premeditated murder. He struggled to come up with an excuse that a jury might find plausible. But with little success. He watched Tucka bustle about the DeRosenquill living room, babbling to herself about auction prices and resale values.

"I could feel at home here!" she said, upending an enamel urn to check the bottom for a price tag. "What about you?"

Before Killium could answer, Primm arrived, wheeling her father before her.

Tucka strode to meet them with her hand elegantly out-stretched before her.

Primm took one look at Tucka—in her too-low, too-tight coatdress, her beehive hairdo with the black widow ornament, and her overly lush vicious red lips—and took an instant dislik-ing to her. Tucka took one look at Primm—in her worn overalls and rubber workboots—and the feeling was mutual.

However, the reaction between Tucka and Androse was profoundly different.

"You must know why we're here," Tucka began. "That ghastly business at Reezor's. We've obviously got an epidemic on our hands. And the committee wants to act quickly to, shall we say, nip it in the bud." She and Androse both chuckled at her wit.

"I don't see—" Primm began, but Androse cut her off.

"How can we help?" he asked. He rolled himself closer to Tucka and looked up at her with the same fiery DeRosenquill eyes that had been the undoing of many a Thorny End maiden.

"We're making a comprehensive survey," Tucka began. "This is Mr. Lintoncloff, my associate."

It was Primm's turn to interrupt.

"I thought his name was Clovlinnik. Tarp distinctly said 'Clovlinnik.' And he never makes a mistake."

Tucka didn't miss a beat. "It's hyphenated. Clovlinnik-Lintoncloff. But that's a mouthful, don't you think?" She turned to Androse for support.

"Primm, don't be so prickly," he said. "This is serious busi-ness."

"I just can't help wondering what business it is of hers."

"Primm!" Androse scolded. "Why don't you make Mr. Linencloth a drink?"

"Yes, Father," she said.

"Now, what can we do to help?" Androse returned his full attention to Tucka.

Tucka took command of his wheelchair and rolled him toward the fireplace, away from Primm's prying ears.

Chapter 64
BACK TO THE DRAWING BOARD

"I've got to hand it to you," Hermux told Terfle. "That was brilliant."

"It was better than brilliant," Linka added. "It was stupendous."

"You're the bomb!" Twigg said.

Terfle beamed. It *had* been a bit of daring ingenuity on her part. Who would have guessed that the queen bee had never had her portrait done before? Naturally, Terfle thought, it had been an exceedingly flattering portrait. And that had been followed by an entire suite of drawings showing the royals and their life-style in the best light possible. So of course, when her friends arrived, as Terfle knew they would, their reception had been as cordial as the bees could manage, considering their militaristic worldview.

"They had us completely fooled," Hermux said. "Even Tucka thought they were going to attack. She couldn't watch!"

Fortunately Terfle couldn't speak or she would have had to admit that she hadn't been able to watch either. She wasn't sure what the bees would do.

"My dad's dead," Twigg burst out indignantly. "It's their

fault, and Tucka and that other mouse didn't even say they're sorry!"

"*We're* sorry, Twigg," Linka told him. She put her arm around him. "And they won't get away with it. You can count on that."

"Right!" agreed Hermux. "And the first order of business is putting a stop to their scheme. They're up to something big. I can tell. Who wants to help?"

Everyone raised their hand.

"All right," Hermux said. "Where do we begin?"

"It would certainly be easier to stop their scheme if we knew what it was," Linka commented. "I suggest we search the lab for clues."

Hermux started with Killium's desk. Linka went through the lab equipment and chemicals. Twigg rummaged through the storeroom. And Terfle performed a systematic aerial reconnaissance of both rooms and their contents.

Twigg appeared in the door to the storeroom, holding two metal tanks with back straps and hoses. Each tank was marked with a skull and crossbones. "What do you think these are?"

Linka took one look. "His and hers poison sprayers, I'd say. But for what?"

"Maybe they're going to use them to rob a bank!" said Twigg.

"That doesn't sound quite like Tucka," Linka said.

Terfle signaled that she'd found something too. She had noticed it on her flyby of the whiteboard. Something had been written there and erased. But it was difficult to read.

Twigg played with the whiteboard, rotating it in its stand until the light hit it just right to reveal faint traces of writing. He read it to the others.

gardenias   fresh-baked chocolate chip cookies

jasmine   coffee

lilies   toast

sweet peas   popcorn

                   babies

"Is it a shopping list?" asked Hermux.

"I don't think so," Linka said. "You don't buy babies. And what would Tucka do with one, anyway?"

Hermux shook his head. "Too scary to think about. And what do you this is?" He handed around a sheet of paper. "I found it on Killium's desk."

"Looks like a drawing of a rose," Linka said.

"Looks more like a map to me," Twigg argued. "It says north and south right here."

"Oh my gosh!" said Linka. "You're right, Twigg. It's a map. I totally missed that."

Twigg smiled.

"But why a map of a rose?" Linka mused.

Hermux slapped his forehead. "I think I know! The police report! Remember? This morning? Dead roses at Reezor's place. It's a map of Reezor's garden. He told me about it. It's shaped like a rose. They killed his roses!"

"But why?" asked Linka.

"I don't know."

Linka frowned. "And where are they going tonight? Tucka said they had important business to attend to."

"I have no idea," Hermux admitted. "Predicting Tucka is like trying to predict a hurricane." The excitement of Terfle's return and their narrow escape from the bees was beginning to fade. Hermux found himself suddenly tired. He slumped back against the whiteboard and caught himself just in time when it flipped over in its stand.

The whiteboard made a half revolution and came to stop. There on the other side was Killium's map of the Villa DeRosenquill.

Chapter 65
ESTATE PLANNING

Androse DeRosenquill had always relied on two things to raise his spirits—the presence of a beautiful woman and the chance to show off his roses. When Tucka Mertslin appeared on his doorstep and asked to see his acreage of *Rosa fragrantissima,* it felt like the arrival of a guardian angel in answer to a secret prayer. For more than a day he had been tormented by waves of guilt and rage. The guilt—over his role in Plank's disappearance and his wife's broken heart—he had managed to hide from himself and the world for all these many years. The rage was against Hermux, who had meddled in matters that did not concern him and who might yet create a scandal that could disgrace him and the DeRosenquill name forever. Escorting the glamorous Miss Mertslin on a personal tour of his roses was the perfect antidote to both guilt and worry.

As for Tucka, the encounter with Androse was proving invigorating as well. She found Androse irresistibly elegant and masculine, and the wheelchair, with its hint of vulnerability, only added to his appeal. Tucka preferred a certain degree of vulnerability in a man. Especially a rich man. And just how rich

Androse was began to be obvious to her when they arrived at their destination.

Androse had taken them to the family pavilion, a marble structure that looked out over the valley.

"I come here alone sometimes to think," Androse said. "And *these* are the *fragrantissimas*." He pointed out beyond the columns, down the broad marble steps to the sweeping beds of roses that descended toward the river. It was nearly dark by then, but the view was still majestic. "Did I tell you how I developed the *fragrantissima*?"

"Twice," Tucka responded. "You own all this?"

"Clear to the river. It's all DeRosenquill land."

"DeRosenquill and Son," she mused. "He's a very lucky boy."

"Sadly"—and for a moment Androse did look genuinely sad—"there is no son."

When Primm and Killium reached the pavilion, Tucka regarded her with new interest. Tucka had a fine legal mind and had used it on more than one occasion. When it came to inheritance, she told herself, placing a hand protectively on Androse's shoulder, surely a wife would trump a daughter. Particularly a dull, unattractive one.

"Do tell us again how you developed the *fragrantissima*," she said. "It's such a beautiful story. And so romantic. The quest for the perfect rose! It would make a wonderful opera."

"Do you like opera?" Androse asked.

"Like it? I have box seats. You'll have to come up sometime. Next month is *The Gypsy Moth*. We'll make an evening of it. Just the two of us." She rubbed his shoulder suggestively. "You've got a knot there. You've been working too hard, haven't you?"

"It goes with the territory," he said. "Whatever you're doing, don't stop. It feels wonderful."

Tucka rubbed harder. "People tell me I have magic fingers."

And then Androse spoiled the moment.

"Mertslin?" he said quizzically. "It's a funny name, isn't it? I don't recognize it. Is that one of the old families?"

Tucka stopped her massage. "Old enough," she said. She pointed out at the fields. "So these are the roses that supply Reezor Bleesom with his precious rose oil?"

"One hundred percent of it," Androse said proudly. "Those fields of his were just for show. They wouldn't have gone into production for two or three more years."

"Did you hear that, Killium?" Tucka asked. "We've got to do everything possible to protect these fields. Poor Reezor would be positively ruined if anything were ever to happen to them."

"I'm sorry, Mr. Tantamoq, but Mr. DeRosenquill and Miss Primm cannot be disturbed. They're with a delegation from the Emergency Committee to Save the Roses."

"A tall mouse with a black widow in her hair?" asked Linka.

"The very woman," Tarp said.

"That's Miss Mertslin," explained Hermux. "She's the chairwoman. She appointed me treasurer just this afternoon."

"And I'm the secretary," said Linka. "Isn't that typical? This is Twigg. He's the head of our youth group. And this, you may remember, is Terfle." She pointed out the Sport-a-Pet that Twigg wore. "She's handling our natural pest control program. Sorry we're late!"

"No one told me to expect you," Tarp said.

"Miss Mertslin has a lot on her mind right now," Linka said. "Where is everyone?"

"Mr. Androse is showing them the *fragrantissima* plantings."

"Of course," said Hermux. "They would want to see them right away. How do we get there?"

Tarp's directions were clear and simple. From the house it was a ten-minute walk. They managed it in five. The family pavilion was a private refuge from the busy workings of the DeRosenquill nurseries. A tall boxwood hedge protected it from view. The only entrance was through a gate in the hedge. They paused there to reconnoiter.

The moon had risen by now. The pavilion glowed pale against the darkness beyond it. Four figures were visible among the columns.

"That's them," whispered Hermux. "What should we do?"

"We've got to stall them long enough to figure out what their plan is," Linka whispered back. "They can't very well shoot us in front of the DeRosenquills."

"Twigg, you and Terfle stay here out of sight. We may need backup. And remember, you can't trust Tucka, no matter what she says. And believe me, she'll say anything."

"Don't worry," Twigg responded. "I've got her number."

Then Hermux and Linka stepped out of the shadows and walked toward the pavilion.

"Sorry we're late!" Hermux called out in greeting. "I hope we didn't miss anything important."

"Hermux? Linka? Is that you?" Primm was surprised to see them arrive at that hour.

Tucka was shocked to see them arrive at all.

And Killium was simply numb. He had never seen ghosts before.

"Tantamoq!" Tucka declared. *"Quelle surprise!"*

Androse was angry. "Tantamoq!" he snorted. "I told you you were fired!"

"Dad! That's no way to talk," Primm chided. "Hermux, what's wrong?"

"The Emergency Committee to Save the Roses is what's wrong. Have they spelled out the details of their spraying program? We hear it got real results at Reezor's!" Hermux announced.

"What do you mean by that?" Androse asked. He wheeled his chair away from Tucka. "What results? Those roses were dead as doornails."

"That was the intention," said Hermux. Their hunch had been right.

"Don't listen to Tantamoq!" Tucka commanded Androse. "I've known him for years, and you can't trust him."

"I don't trust him!" Androse said. "But what's this about spray?"

"It's nothing!" Tucka said.

"They're planning to spray your roses and kill them," Linka said flat out. "That's what they did at Reezor's. It's all part of their plot to put Reezor Bleesom out of business."

"That sounds pretty far-fetched," said Androse.

"And that's only the beginning!" Hermux added.

"Of course it's far-fetched," Tucka said. She sounded like the very voice of reason. She extended both her arms and turned slowly in place for Androse's benefit. "Do you see any hidden sprayers?"

Androse shook his head.

"They're both nutcases!" Tucka said. "Next they'll be trying to tell you that we held them prisoner in a secret lab and tried to kill them with wild bees."

"Tantamoq, I had you pegged for a nut to begin with," Androse concluded. "Primm! I want you to escort these people off our property. Right now!"

"You don't want to know happened to Plank?" Hermux asked.

"Of course we do!" Primm said.

"NO, WE DO NOT!" Androse intervened. "Anything this mouse says is nothing but slander and blackmail! I forbid you to listen to a single word. Now get him out of here. And her too! And if they give you any trouble, call the police!"

"You're making a terrible mistake!" Hermux told Androse.

From the corner of his eye Hermux saw Tucka open her purse and remove a bottle of perfume. As she held it up and prepared to spray herself with fragrance, something about it seemed wrong to Hermux. A ray of moonlight glinted on the bottle, revealing Reezor Bleesom's golden monogram. There was no way on earth that Tucka Mertslin would wear one of Reezor's perfumes.

Hermux leapt forward and swatted the bottle from her hand.

"The poison's in the perfume!" he shouted to Linka. "Get that bottle and don't let it break!"

Linka, whose profession as an adventuress required fast re-flexes and considerable athletic ability, sprang after the flying bottle. She executed a rolling fall, caught the bottle one-handed, and scrambled back to her feet.

"Got it!" she said. "Safe and sound!"

Chapter 67

MERRILY WE ROLL ALONG

Linka read the bottle's label. "Time to Smell the Roses by Reezor Bleesom. Now that is a surprise!"

"This is outrageous!" Androse fumed. "You two can't barge in here and rough up my guests. You'll leave immediately or I'll press charges! I have connections at City Hall and I won't hesitate to use them."

Tucka moved to Androse's side as though placing herself under his protection. "Before you go, would you be so kind as to return my perfume, Ms. Perflinger?"

"Oh, I think not," said Linka, pocketing the bottle. "For now we'll just keep it as evidence."

Killium pointed his gun at Linka. "Give the lady her perfume!" Hermux and Linka weren't ghosts after all. Somehow they had survived the bees. He was relieved that he wasn't a murderer after all. But if they talked, he and Tucka would still go to prison. And now they had evidence. The pistol seemed like the obvious solution.

"Good boy!" said Tucka. She stretched her hand out to Linka. "I'll take that now."

Linka looked to Hermux. But when Killium moved the gun

to cover him, she conceded defeat and surrendered the perfume bottle. With a grand gesture Tucka reached for it, her luscious lips parted in a smile of victory. But before her fingers closed on their prize, she snatched her hand back with a spastic jerk.

"Ouch!" she squawked. She blew on her fingers. "That hurt!"

"Bee sting?" Hermux asked. He had watched the stone strike its target perfectly.

Killium saw it too. But before he could register what it was, a sharp metallic ping sounded. He screamed as he was hit too, and he dropped the gun.

For a moment no one moved. Then Hermux, Linka, Tucka, and Killium dove for the gun. While they struggled on the ground, Primm commandeered her father's wheelchair.

"Let's get you back to the house!" she said. "We'll call the police from there. And they can straighten this out!" She began to wheel him back toward the gate, but she found the path blocked by Twigg, slingshot in hand.

"Where do you think you're going?" he asked.

"Get out of our way, you young ruffian!" Androse said. "We know how to deal with trespassers here!"

But Twigg was not to be intimidated. He herded Primm and Androse back toward the pavilion, where they found that the fight on the ground had boiled down to Hermux and Killium. They rolled this way and that in a flurry of dust while Tucka and Linka each watched for an opening to jump in on her partner's side. Suddenly there was a retching noise. Hermux's body twisted away wildly. He pushed himself free of Killium and clambered to his feet, brushing his face and chest frantically.

"Ugggh!" he said.

Killium got to his feet, panting hard but holding the gun.

"What happened?" Linka asked.

Hermux pointed at Killium accusingly. "He threw up on me!"

Killium tossed a torn plastic packet on the ground. "Score one for fake vomit!" he taunted. Keeping the others covered with his gun, he backed his way carefully across the pavilion and rejoined Tucka where she was repairing the damage to her beehive hairdo. She pinned the black widow back into place, and then, as she had many times before in her life, she took charge of the situation.

"Everybody please shut up for moment while I think!" she said.

Twigg answered her with a perfectly placed shot in her beehive. It exploded in a shower of fake fur and spider legs. Tucka turned to Killium. "Will you please shoot that little monster! I have never seen such an ill-behaved child in my entire life!"

Killium took aim at Twigg. Twigg aimed right back.

"You want to go down for cold-blooded murder?" Hermux asked. "There'll be witnesses!"

"Not for long!" countered Tucka. "Besides, it's self-defense. He attacked us."

"He's just a boy, and you attacked first!" said Linka.

"Did not!" said Tucka.

"Did too!"

"Tell it to my lawyers!" Tucka said. "Shoot!"

"Stop them!" Hermux implored Androse.

"Why me?" Androse complained. "I don't even know the boy!"

Hermux had mixed feelings about revealing Twigg's identity to Androse. Androse hadn't been a very good father in

Hermux's books. And who knew what kind of grandfather he would make. But right then there wasn't time to be picky or diplomatic. Hermux blurted it out. "Because he's your grandson, you selfish fool!"

"My grandson?" said Androse. He searched Twigg's face.

"Plank's boy!" Hermux shouted.

"Father!" Primm cried. "Did you hear that?"

Tucka's nerves had reached the point of no return. "Will you please shoot somebody!" she screamed.

Killium had been ready to fire. Right up until all the talk about sons and grandsons. Now his willpower wavered. Tucka was smart. There was no doubting that. She was smart enough to get away with shooting Androse DeRosenquill's grandson. But then a thought occurred to him—it wasn't Tucka who was pulling the trigger, was it?

Exasperated, Tucka slapped Killium on the back.

As the gun went off, Androse jumped from his wheelchair and took two steps forward. He also took the bullet intended for his grandson.

He collapsed, and Primm broke into a wail.

Hermux crouched behind Androse's wheelchair and pushed. He steered it straight for Killium. Killium managed two wild shots as the wheelchair picked up speed. Then it struck, scooping him off his feet. Hermux propelled the chair across the pavilion and launched it into space. It careened down the marble stairs and catapulted Killium out over the terraced fields. Moments later he landed with a thud and a moan. He was stuck like Velcro to a sturdy row of roses.

"Welcome to Thorny End," said Hermux. He turned back to the pavilion. Androse DeRosenquill lay on the ground, breathing heavily. Linka and Primm knelt at his side.

259

"He'll be okay," Linka pronounced. "The bullet just grazed his shoulder."

"That shot was meant for me," Twigg told Hermux soberly.

"I know."

"Is he really my grandfather?"

"He is. And that's your aunt. Her name is Primm. She's a nice woman."

Hermux looked around and realized that Tucka was gone. He spotted her crossing the lawn. She was walking very quickly toward the gate.

"You're going to jail for this, Tucka!" he yelled after her.

"Don't be ridiculous!" she called back. "You can't prove I was ever here!"

Her pace quickened. Then, without any warning, her legs buckled beneath her and she collapsed, yelping with pain.

Twigg lowered his slingshot.

"Remember that," he told Hermux, grinning with a satisfaction. "The back of the knee is very tender."

Chapter 68
A Picture Is Worth a
Thousand Words

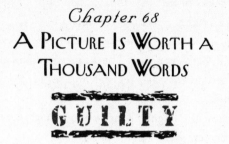

The week had been hot. Friday morning dawned warm, promising another scorcher of a day. But shortly after lunch a July thunderstorm swept through Pinchester, leaving the city washed clean and hung out to dry in bright, fresh sunshine. Nip propped the shop door open to take advantage of the cool mountain air that the storm had left behind. Then he set out the coffee. And the donuts. Two for Hermux, who, since his return from Thorny End, had stuck firmly to his new diet. And four for Nip, who was blessed with high metabolism, strong teeth, and a worry-free attitude about life.

Hermux was in the back at his bench. Bratchlin Weffup had brought in a remarkable antique wristwatch he'd gotten at an auction. It had a bell that rang the hours, the quarters, and the minutes. Or at least it had at one time. And it would again when Hermux had finished with it. There was still much to be done. The mechanism was extremely complex. It was painstaking work, and Hermux was enjoying it immensely.

"Coffee break!" Nip announced.

Hermux put down his loupe and his tools and joined Nip at the front counter. He began with his old favorite—the plain chocolate cake donut.

"Read it again," Hermux said.

"That makes three times today," said Nip.

"That's all right. This one's for Terfle."

Terfle was standing at her easel. Hermux waved up at her. Paintbrush in hand, she waved back. Hermux had cleared space on a shelf behind the cash register and set up a small painting studio for her.

"All right," Nip began. "Once upon a time, in a faraway city called Pinchester, there was a trial . . ."

TABLES TURN AT CELEBRITY TRIAL—

Mertslin Enters Plea Bargain After Jury Views New Evidence

PINCHESTER, July 8—The courtroom was packed again at the sensational trial of cosmetics tycoon and superspokesmodel Tucka Mertslin on charges of accessory to manslaughter, criminal negligence, criminal mischief, vandalism, and attempted murder in the shooting attack on Androse DeRosenquill, patriarch of the DeRosenquill rose dynasty.

Throughout two weeks of grueling testimony, Mertslin protested her innocence, repeatedly interrupting prosecution witnesses to appeal directly to the jury. "I am the victim here," she reminded jurors tearfully. "I am the victim of an overzealous prosecutor, a rogue employee, and a ruthless private detective with a personal grudge against me—whom I intend to sue for every cent he has just as soon as you fair and impartial people dismiss these trumped-up charges against me."

Indeed, the jury, many of whom have been seen carrying Tucka Mertslin gift bags home from the courthouse each day, seemed prepared to acquit Miss Mertslin on all charges.

Then today the prosecution called its last witness, Terfle (no last name), a professional associate of Hermux Tantamoq, the watchmaker and detective who has figured prominently in the case. Jurors were shown eyewitness drawings made by Terfle at the scene of the crime on the night in question. The drawings offered graphic proof that Mertslin was a willing participant in the events that led to DeRosenquill's shooting and not a hostage of her employee Dr. Killium Wollar, as she has claimed.

Mertslin's attorneys requested

an immediate recess. The plea bar-
gain was announced two hours later.
The terms will not be made public, although unconfirmed reports
suggest a combination of financial
compensation for the victims and
unspecified community service for
Ms. Mertslin.

Miss Mertslin could not be
reached for comment.

When Nip finished, Hermux asked, "Well, Terfle? Does that
sound right? Professional associate?"

Terfle curtsied.

"Professional associate of what?" asked Linka. She breezed
through the open door, her arms full of packages.

"Of *whom*," said Hermux. "And it's me. What have you
got there?"

"Oh, this and that!" Linka responded. She gave him a peck
on the cheek. "I picked up a few bargains at Orsik and Arrbale.
They're having a big summer sale. Hi, Nip! Hi, Terfle! How's
the new portrait coming?"

Terfle shrugged. Oil paints were difficult to master.

"I picked up something for you too." Linka put the smallest
package next to Hermux's saucer of donuts. When he reached
for it, she whisked the remaining donut away and bit into it.

"Mmmm," she said. "I think Lanayda's finally got it." On his
first day back in the shop, Hermux had described the cherry-
rosehip-peanut cruller to Lanayda in glowing detail, and she had
been trying out recipes ever since.

Hermux unwrapped the package.

264

"It's not a present," Linka cautioned. "It's just a little something."

It was a bottle of Fresh Mown Hay cologne by Reezor Bleesom.

"He signed it for you."

And he had.

> To my friend Hermux,
>   With gratitude,
>   Reezor

"Thank you, dear!" said Hermux as the phone rang. "Hermux Tantamoq Watchmaker. May I help you?"

It was Androse DeRosenquill.

"Tantamoq!" he blustered. "I believe we still have some business to attend to. I want you here tomorrow morning! No later than ten."

Hermux hesitated.

"That is, of course," Androse continued on a slightly humbler note, "if it's convenient for you. Linka and Terfle too. Primm will meet you at the airport."

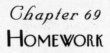

Chapter 69
HOMEWORK

Business was booming again in Thorny End. With all the publicity surrounding Killium's and Tucka's trials, tourism was up. Way up. The inn was fully booked. The airport was crowded. The airline had added an extra flight each day to and from Pinchester. The shops at the market were busy selling rose soaps, rose oils, rose calendars, rose candies, and roses too, of course. Even the taxidermist Thirxen Ghoulter has seen a big bump in his business. His new line of black widow jewelry and hair ornaments was proving very popular. The black widows were plastic, but realistic and very affordable.

Apparently things had changed at DeRosenquill & Son as well. When Primm picked them up at the airport, she was driving the institute's old van. It bore a new logo:

DeRosenquill & Family, Thorny End

Linka pointed it out to Hermux.

"Go, Primm!" he said.

The second obvious change was Primm herself. She seemed noticeably younger and more relaxed.

"Father wants to see you right away," she said. "I hope you can stay for lunch. I've planned a picnic."

"We'd love to," said Linka. "How is your father?"

"He's making a remarkable recovery. He's the same. But different. You'll see."

"And Twigg?" Hermux asked. He knew Terfle would want to know.

"Twigg is—" Primm shook her head and smiled. "Twigg is himself. You'll see that too."

"And you?" Linka asked.

"I am— I am— I guess you could say that I am amazed." She laughed. "Yes. I think that about sums it up." She headed through town and turned toward the waterfront.

"Aren't we meeting your father?" Hermux asked.

"Oh, Father's not at home anymore," she said. "You'll see."

As they passed the courthouse, Linka elbowed Hermux. A sign on the sidewalk announced that Tucka Mertslin, the world's beauty authority, would be there every day the following week dispensing free beauty advice from 9:00 A.M. to 5:00 P.M. No appointment necessary.

"I guess that's what she considers public service," said Linka.

"It's probably the best she can do," said Hermux. "At least she can't hurt anyone."

"Sometimes I wonder about that." Linka laughed.

The ferry was waiting for them, and Primm drove straight on board.

"Father retired," she told them. "If you can call it that. He's

267

moved out to the island. Tucka deeded it back as part of her settlement."

When the ferry pulled into Jeckel Island, Twigg was waiting for them at the dock. He wore farmer's overalls and a straw hat. But he still had his combat boots. And spikes of fur stuck out here and there from the hat.

"Hermux!" he said.

"Twigg!" Hermux gave him a warm hug. "Look at you! You're a farmer!"

"Yeah, I guess," Twigg said. He embraced Linka awkwardly.

"You look wonderful," she told him warmly. "I love the hat."

"Didn't Terfle come?" he asked.

"Of course she came!" Hermux said.

At that very moment Terfle landed on Twigg's hat.

"Hey, Terfle!" Twigg put his paw up and she crawled aboard.

"She brought a whole new sketchbook of drawings to show you," Hermux said. "And she's painting in oils now."

Primm handed Twigg the keys to the van. "You drive," she told him. "But take it slow."

With Terfle perched on his shoulder, Twigg drove them very slowly and very carefully up the lane to the house.

Androse met them in his wheelchair on the front lawn. The house and the garden were a construction site. Androse was surrounded by carpenters, painters, masons, and gardeners. They were all talking at once. When he saw Primm and her passengers arrive, he threw up his hands and announced, "You'll all get your answers now. Talk to the boss."

Hermux's eyebrows shot up. A whole lot had changed at DeRosenquill & Family.

The workers surged toward them, drawings and plans in hand, barking questions left and right.

Hermux and Linka stepped out of Primm's way. But Primm followed right along, and the workers rushed past her and surrounded Twigg.

A large squirrel in overalls pushed his way close to the front. "Boss!" he shouted at Twigg. "Boss!" He gestured proudly at his hard hat. FOREMAN, it said in a crude scrawl. "What do you think?"

Hermux recognized him then. It was Hanger. Next to him stood Skuhl. His hard hat said ASSISTANT FOREMAN.

"How about it?" Hanger insisted. He nodded toward Skuhl. "We make a great team!"

Twigg covered his ears. "Stop yelling at me!" he said.

The yelling ceased.

Twigg uncovered his ears. "I'm busy right now, so talk to him!" He pointed at Androse, and the workers' migration began again.

As Hanger scrambled by, he caught sight of Hermux. He broke his stride for a split second and tipped his hard hat. "No hard feelings!" he said cheerfully. "You gotta think positive!" Then he raced away. "Boss! I'm a born leader! How about it?"

Androse shrugged. "I'll think it over," he said. Then he called to Hermux and Linka, "I guess I'm still needed for something around here." He managed a brief wave before he was engulfed by the crowd.

"It's a little game they play," Primm explained. "Father gave the island to Twigg. Twigg gave it back to him. And so on.

Nobody knows which one's boss. But I'm starting to have my suspicions."

"Who?" asked Hermux, curious.

"Not my father," she answered. "For a change."

"I see," said Hermux.

"And we have you and Linka and Terfle to thank for that."

"I hope that's good," said Linka.

"Oh, it's very good. I think we're all growing up at last."

Chapter 70
HOME IS WHERE THE HEART IS

Of all the things that had changed, perhaps the tree house had the most to show for it.

What was broken had been fixed. The rungs on the ladder. The windowpanes. The boards in the floor. What was missing was now there. Two new walls. A door and a balcony. A bed. A table. Chairs. A cupboard. What was bare had been painted. It was a home in the sky.

"My first home ever," Twigg bragged. "Dad built it. And Grandad and I fixed it up."

"Grandad?" Hermux asked.

"I call him Mr. DeRosenquill to his face," Twigg said.

"I guess that's more respectful," commented Linka.

"No," Twigg said. "It irritates him. Now he calls me Mr. DeRosenquill too. I like that. I've never been a mister before."

"And he gave you the island?" Hermux inquired. "That's a surprise."

"So he says." Twigg shrugged.

"And you gave it back?" Linka asked.

"I told him he could live here *if* he didn't try to boss me around. He's putting a ramp on the house for his wheels."

"What are you going to do here?" Hermux asked.

"I'm not sure," said Twigg. "Maybe a summer camp for kids like me. Grandad hates that idea." Twigg laughed. "Of course he wants me to breed roses. He's going to show me how to make a rose with super-big thorns."

"Who would want roses with extra-big thorns?" Linka asked.

"I don't know," Twigg admitted. "But I'm going to call it Tyrannosaurus Rose! Won't that be cool?"

Terfle thought so.

"And we're going to build a memorial for Dad in the rose garden." Twigg grew serious. He walked to the new window that faced the house. "That's where he's buried." He pointed.

Linka joined him at the window. "We're really sad about your dad."

"I know," said Twigg. "We all are. He didn't have a very good life, did he?"

"He had a very good son," Hermux told him. "That's more than some people get."

Twigg remembered something. "We may have a rock festival too!"

"There you go!" said Hermux. "Your dad would have liked that."

"Grandad says over his dead body. And Aunt Primm says he'll outlive us all. I want to open an amusement park. I'm already working on the first ride—the Tunnel of Death!"

Terfle rang her bell enthusiastically.

"You want to see it?" Twigg asked.

"Why don't you and Terfle go ahead," Linka suggested. "Hermux and I will catch up with you."

"Primm was right," Linka said when they had gone. "It's

all amazing." She opened the door and stepped out onto the brand-new balcony. Hermux joined her there. A sliver of ocean was visible through the trees. And from the ocean blew a steady cool breeze.

"It's hard to believe it's the same island," he said.

"No guns."

"No spiders."

"No danger."

"I hope we don't get bored."

"We can't," Linka promised. "There's a picnic!"

"The truth is, I couldn't get bored," said Hermux.

"No?" she asked. "Why not?"

Hermux took her hand. "Because you're here." Then he pulled her into his arms and kissed her.